Maverick

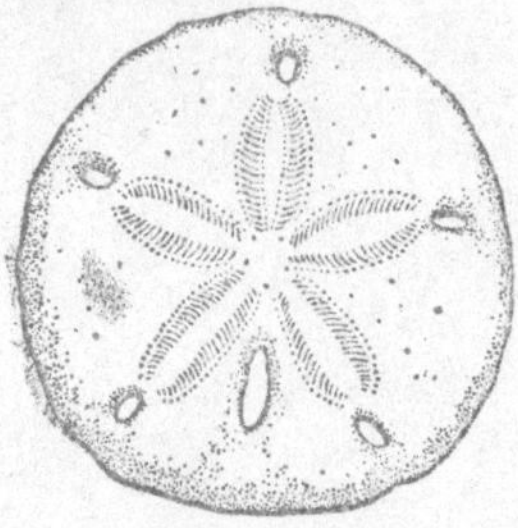

G·K Hall &Co.
Large Print

This Large Print Book carries the Seal of Approval of N.A.V.H.

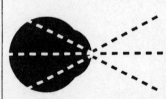

MAVERICK

Verne Athanas

G.K. Hall & Co.
Thorndike, Maine

Published in Large Print by arrangement with Golden West Literary Agency in association with Laurence Pollinger, Ltd.

G.K. Hall Large Print Book Series.

Typeset in 16 pt. Plantin.

Printed on acid free paper in Great Britain.

Library of Congress Cataloging-in-Publication Data

Athanas, Verne.
Maverick / by Verne Athanas.
p. cm.
ISBN 0-8161-5838-X (alk. paper : lg. print)
1. Large type books. I. Title.
[PS3551.T39M38 1993]813′.54—dc20 93-25507
CIP

AUTHOR'S DEDICATION—

This one is for Minnie, because she liked it the first time round.

CHAPTER ONE

Clay Lanahan heard Jed Martindale coming, a quarter-mile away in the still dark. It was as faint as a distant prairie wolf's yell, but no prairie wolf went '*Hoooo-o-o-ha-a-ah!*' in that quavering tenor tone. It was Jed, all right, and when he yelled like that he was drunk. Clay almost resignedly hunched himself forward and up and over to the wood pile to freshen the fire under the coffeepot. Then he stood a moment listening for the bell on the mare with the horse herd yonder, finally heard it, and decided he'd wait for Jed to come before he made another circle.

Jed was a long time coming. The fresh wood flared and burned brightly and subsided into the general heap of glowing coals which was the campfire. Finally, not quite uneasy, Clay got up again, walked out of the fire glow and into the dark. He buttoned his sheepskin coat and shrugged the woolly collar against his neck, feeling the wind's wet chill as soon as he left the fire and the tarp windbreak.

It was probably another fifteen minutes before Jed arrived. He came on a slow-walking horse, very quietly, pulled up just outside the circle of firelight and got down in a squeaking of leather and a jingle of metal and a soggy thud as his boots hit the wet earth. Lanahan tossed a couple of dry branching sticks on the fire. The firelit circle surged and expanded, and Jed came waveringly forward, into the light, stopped, planted his feet, and gave Lanahan a wide, wet-eyed staring look.

'A' right,' he said. 'Go on. Say 't. I'm a goddamn fool. Oughta be shot. Gwan, say 't, dammit. Damn dirty skunk. Oughta be shot.'

He was about as colorless as a man can get, Jed Martindale. He was almost twice Lanahan's age, which was twenty-six; the first impression was that he'd weathered gray all over, hair and eyes and clothing and all; he looked mussed and rumpled now, with his lank gray forelock showing under a hat carelessly rammed on his head so that the brim angled back and the crown was caved in on one side. He was drunk but no more remarkable for it; it was a common, ordinary, gray drunk, without the belligerence of a fighting drunk or the drooling of a crying jag, or even the sloppy, witless helplessness of a falling-down drunk. He was just drunk.

'Gwan,' he said. 'Say 't.'

Lanahan said dryly, 'You tell me what, and I'll say it. You haven't given me any shootin' grounds yet, but I'll keep it in mind. Come on and get out of the cold. The coffee's hot.'

'Dwanny coffee. I brung you a drunk.' He reached inside his blanket coat and brought out a quart bottle. Perhaps an inch of amber-tinted whisky sloshed in the bottom. Jed peered at it owlishly. 'God damn,' he said, 'it sure went down fast.' He took two careful steps and held it out. 'Gwan,' he said, 'take a drink, pardner.'

Lanahan resignedly accepted the bottle, twisted the cork squeakingly out, and took a modest drink. The stuff was warm against his teeth and searing hot on its way to his belly; then it subsided to a pervading warmth as he slapped the cork in again.

Jed watched with a careful drunken concentration and as the cork went home in the neck of the bottle, he took a deep breath and said in a blurting stream of words, 'I loss the money Clay gimme a drink.'

Lanahan lowered the bottle to his side. 'You lost what money?'

'Loss the stud money, dammit. I sole 'im all right, an' I got the money, an' he said less have a drink on it, so I had a drink on it, and there was this bunch sittin' roun' the store, an' I bought one, an' they said did I wanta set in on the stud game an' I done it an' I loss the money. Two hundred an' fifty-three dollars an' fifty cents. The three dollars an' fifty cents was mine.'

Lanahan let that soak in, hoping against

hope it wasn't so, but knowing as he looked at Jed that it was so. Inside him the warmth turned to an anger that was momentarily so strong and cold that it was all he could do to hold himself from striking out; and then he saw through the drunken glaze on Jed's face, and knew that drunk or no, Jed was eaten with the miseries of guilt and shame, and anger wouldn't help. But still it was rough, and a little of it showed in his voice as he said brusquely, 'All right, it's done. Get some coffee into you.'

Jed walked with careful concentration to the canvas windbreak, turned and bent his knees and collapsed cross-legged, stared into the fire, and rubbed his thick, chapped, ungloved hands together. 'Doan deserve no coffee,' he said.

'Oh, shut up,' said Lanahan not quite disgustedly. He walked around Jed, cached the bottle behind the tarpaulin, and went to the fire to fill a tin cup from the coffeepot. 'Drink it down,' he said. 'Did you get drunk before, or after?'

Jed held the cup in both hands, warming his palms and fingers on the hot metal. He said without looking up, 'After, I guess. They jus' ast me, an'—ah, hell!'

'Yeah,' said Lanahan. 'Drink that down and roll in.'

'I kin nighthawk it,' said Jed.

'Like hell,' said Lanahan. 'Roll in.'

Jed blinked and scrubbed his face roughly with his wide callused palm. He fumbled the buttons of his coat apart as the fire warmth soaked through. His lids drooped. He straightened out his crossed legs and presented his boots to the fire, as he leaned back on his braced elbows. He yawned widely, his eyes unmoving on the hypnotic flicker of tiny red and yellow and blue flames winking through the coals. 'Damn,' he said to no one in particular, and a minute later he was asleep, inert and unmoving as a log. Lanahan sat and stared broodingly into the fire.

After a while he roused himself to go out to his picketed night horse, and made a slow circle around the quiet horse herd. The stud horse was no great loss, but their grubstake from his sale was; it nearly knocked a good plan and a year's hard work in the head. He rode back to the fire, and found his own bed. He did not sleep well.

The camp was scrawny as poverty in the chill morning light. The grub box and tarpaulins and ropes and sawbucks and sundry rigging were used—hard-used—battered and old. Lanahan built up the fire in a silent, almost sullen, cold-morning grouchiness and emptied the grub box for breakfast.

He made coffee by the simple expedient of dumping half a canteen of water into last night's bitter brew and shoving the pot closer to the heat; when the bacon was fried and removed from the pan he dropped a circular biscuit of hardtack, impervious as flint, into the bubbling bacon grease. He shook Jed, roughly but without rancour, until Jed opened sick red-rimmed eyes. 'Can you make it over here for your grub?'

'Reckon,' said Jed hoarsely, and wallowed clumsily out of his bedding. Jed sipped coffee, put down the tin cup, and essayed the building of a cigarette with his thick, shaking fingers. The brown wheat paper tore, and Jed carefully hoarded the makings in one cupped palm while he got out another paper.

Lanahan remembered the cached bottle then; went and got it, brought it back, and thrust it at Jed.

'Might as well kill it,' he said.

Jed looked up, almost beseechingly. 'Aw, hell,' he said.

'Take it,' said Lanahan. Jed looked down and slowly accepted the bottle. He held it in his hand, watching the gentle sloshing of the bare inch of the amber liquid remaining. There was relief in there, of a sort, an anodyne and buffer for his miseries. He sat there a long moment as if savoring it, and then he said clearly and violently, 'Sonofabitch!' and threw the bottle at a thick-butted tree beyond the fire. Liquid and shards spun out in a gleaming spray.

Lanahan said nothing, understanding the act of atonement, rolled his own cigarette, poured a miserly half cup of the black and bitter brew to finish with it, and said finally, 'Don't see much gain in moving again today, do you? Herd's holding close, and there's grass enough.'

'You're callin' it,' said Jed, disinterestedly.

Lanahan smiled faintly, half bitterly, and got up. He rooted his belt and holster out of his bed and swung it around his waist, under his coat.

'All right,' he said, 'you wrangle 'em. I'm going over to the store.'

Jed said not quite certainly, 'Now, look, it was my trouble—you don't need to go...'

'I'm not looking for any trouble,' said Lanahan. 'We've got to have grub.'

It was ten miles to the pole-and-shake shack which was Brown's Store; prices were higher than a cat's back. Lanahan resignedly paid, wordlessly pocketed his scant change, hung the sack of supplies on his saddle horn, and headed back.

He shrugged his neck deeper into the collar of his sheepskin coat as he rode; the clouds were low and scudding before the persistent wind; it could quite possibly snow again tonight.

We could have made it, he thought. It was pretty near a cinch. Not that it was Jed's fault. Jed wasn't a drunk, in the ordinary sense of the word. When he tied one on, she was a red-eyed wonder with a clove hitch in her tail, and would hold him for as much as a year at a time. But he had really ripped it this time.

It had been a mighty pretty dream. They'd worked it out this long while now, nursing nickels and dimes and hoarding dollars, buying, trading, building up a herd of good horses; geldings and mares and the hammer-headed black stud.

They'd taken the stud in lieu of wages from a man named Myers in the Rogue Valley; his conformation wasn't the best, but he had good blood in him. They'd picked up some scrubs and a couple of good grade mares and moved on, spending their hoarded dollars when they had to, trading when they could, up through the Willamette country where they wintered, to the Dalles and out of there as soon as the weather broke, to the Grande Ronde country. He'd grained the stud regularly, to keep him fat and full of vinegar; ridden him regularly to keep him hard and work some of the ginger out of him; he was their ace in the hole, for his sale would buy grub, and they could Siwash it the rest of the way with no cumbersome wagon outfit. All the mares were bred, deliberately late, to foal in the Wyoming. Money on the hoof, most certainly, but not here, where good horses were cheap and plentiful—Ah, hell, why bellyache about it. When a man comes to where he does nothing but yearn about what might have been, he's ready to be patted in the face with a spadeful of dirt—to hell with it!

He cooked up a prodigal meal with the fresh supplies, and even Jed ate heartily. Afterward, Lanahan said, 'What do you think if we trail 'em down to the Baker City country? We ought to get a better price out of some cow outfit moving out. Might even break even.'

Jed said morosely, 'All right with me. You call it.' Then he looked over to see Lanahan's narrow wryly amused smile and had the grace to grin sheepishly. 'All right, so I'm a bonehead from who laid the chunk. I can't help it.'

'Oh, you're a sad case,' agreed Lanahan. 'And you get to ride circle tonight.'

Jed drained his coffee cup and spat out grounds resignedly. 'Well,' he said, 'it ought to get better. It can't get much worse.'

That afternoon a back-country rider coming from the direction of Brown's Store rode in to their fire and had a cup of coffee with them. 'You're T.C. Lanahan? Well, Brown said to tell you there's a man name of Prather wants to see you. He's holdin' a cow outfit down t'other end of the basin.'

Lanahan looked over at Jed. 'Why not?' he said.

CHAPTER TWO

It was full dark before Lanahan found the place. The Grande Ronde made a swing here, a great curving loop across the sweep of the open land. Someone moved by the fire, the only spot of light in the eye-stretching sweep of the land, and the flames caught sparks and flung them spiraling high into the night as more wood was tossed to the flames.

Lanahan rode straight at the fire, sent a hail ahead to warn of his coming. A voice answered him, and he rode on into the circle of firelight.

'This the Prather camp?' he asked.

'That's right,' said one of them around the fire.

He grunted, and swung down, leather chaps flapping beneath his thick sheepskin coat. He dropped a rein and walked away from his horse.

'I'm looking for Mr. Prather,' he said. He hunkered down by the fire and thrust his blunt chapped hands at the flames.

A woman's voice came to him from across the fire, and brought his head up sharply.

'What do you want?' she said. Then she came into the circle of light. She had a shawl over her head, and a long dark coat gathered tightly about her; but he could tell she was young, and, as the light touched her face, he could see she was truly handsome. But the tone she had used on him kept him where he was, not standing, not touching his hat.

'I want to see Mr. Prather,' he said, and his own tone ignored her sex. He saw her lips compress, just a moment's tiny pressure, and then she said, 'My father is ill. If you will tell me your business with him.' She did not let the words trail off. Her lips firmly put a period to the words that were neither question or statement.

He said, 'I'm T.C. Lanahan.'

A dark shape came out of the darkness and resolved itself into a man who stepped into the light and said in rough arrogance, 'And who the hell is T.C. Lanahan?'

Lanahan turned his head slightly to look at the man. He filled out an Army overcoat, with a double row of brass buttons glinting against the dark blue wool, the coat cut off at hip length. His hat was pushed back and the underside of the brim caught the firelight and reflected it onto his broad, wind-reddened face, so that he was squinting a little to look across the flames at Lanahan. His right hand worked a buckskin glove tight over the knuckles of his left.

Lanahan gave him one long, appraising look, then moved his eyes back to the girl.

He said nothing.

The girl was uncertain. It showed in the way her eyes moved back and forth between Lanahan and the other man. The man came around the fire, moving easily, with confidence. 'Your manners are bad,' he said.

The girl said swiftly, 'Homer...'

Lanahan came to his feet, not quickly, but easily, to stand as tall as Homer, though not so heavy even in the bulky sheepskin coat. His three-day stubble of black beard made a little scratching sound on the collar as he turned his head.

'Sorry,' he said shortly, and turned to tramp to his horse.

The girl said, 'But what...'

'It's not important,' said Lanahan. He picked up the trailing rein, and then another voice came from the fire.

'Just a moment, if you please. Were you looking for me, Mr. Lanahan?'

The man was coming around the fire, one hand up to the side of his face to shield off the light, looking out into the darkness where Lanahan was. 'I am Amos Prather,' the man said.

He looked tired, bone-tired, as if he were never really rested. He wore a long overcoat, a city coat, with only a single button fastened, for he wore a heavy sweater and a thick wool muffler under it that made the fitted coat too tight. He put out a hand as

Lanahan dropped the rein again, and turned back. 'I'm happy to make your acquaintance, Mr. Lanahan,' he said.

His hand was narrow and icy cold, and he did not put much pressure into the handshake, but his eyes looked up alertly at Lanahan from under the flat brim of his dark hat.

'You will have to accept my apologies,' Prather went on. 'I have been ill, and I was lying down. If you will come with me, we can talk in the wagon.' Lanahan followed him silently around the fire and back into darkness again.

Amos Prather reached high to pull a little door open, and lamplight spilled down a set of narrow steps at the rear of the wagon. The girl went up, and then Prather's hand urged Lanahan ahead. He stepped up, turned a little sideways to get through the slot of the doorway.

The wagon was built like a sheep wagon, or a gypsy's caravan; the box sides built up waist high, the rest framed like a cabin with two-by-twos, covered with taut canvas so that the top rose to a center ridge like an unceiled cabin. A flowered cretonne curtain cut off the front end of the wagon box, obviously the girl's bed. Most of one side was taken up by another bed, rumpled now, which let down on chains at either end like a jail bunk, so that it could be folded up against the wall when not in use. A plank table that could be used the same way was already raised and secured on the other side. A sheet-iron stove, a couple of box cupboards, a mirror, a small water keg above the wood box—there was room for nothing more.

'Sit down, sit down,' said Prather. He pulled the door shut behind him, gestured to the edge of the bed. 'We are hard put for room,' he said.

The girl pulled the divided cretonne curtain apart a foot or so, and sat on her own bed, looking at them. Lanahan dragged off his hat and sat down gingerly on Prather's bed with Prather beside him. The hanging lamp rocked a little from their motion of climbing in, and the shifting light made a subtly changing pattern in the girl's thick chestnut hair as she lifted the shawl from her head and let it fall across her shoulders.

Prather said in his dry precise voice, 'I somehow expected an older man, Mr. Lanahan.'

Lanahan said mildly, 'I'm old enough.'

'Of course, of course. But, that is neither here nor there. I understand you have had some experience at trailing cattle.'

Lanahan said briefly, 'Three trips up the Chisholm, one of them clear to Fort Kearny. Once from Baker City east to Laramie. Wagon boss on the last two, but you'll have to take my word for it. I don't keep letters.' He loosened the buttons on his sheepskin coat and threw the sides back. The little stove was hot. Amos Prather kept himself bundled up, and held his hands a little out from his knees toward the stove.

'Well, then,' said Amos Prather, 'to business. I am moving two thousand head to the Bighorn country. I'd like to have you handle them for me. I am not a cattle-man, even if I were not ill.'

'What kind of a herd?' asked Lanahan.

Prather was carefully rubbing his narrow hands together. 'You would call it a mixed herd, I suppose.'

'Mixed how?'

A little spot of color came on Prather's bony cheeks. He twisted to look at Lanahan.

'Steers,' he said. 'Two- and three-year old cows.'

'Mixed how?' repeated Lanahan without inflection.

Prather again put his attention to rubbing his hands. 'About seventy-five per cent cows. The steers from yearlings up.'

'Way up, I'll bet,' said Lanahan dryly. Then he added bluntly. 'That's a damn poor herd to trail. And since you didn't mention it, I'll bet the cows are bred.'

'Yes. Most of them, I guess.' He turned his head as a rap came on the door. 'Yes?'

The door swung open without answer,

and the one the girl had called Homer, who thought Lanahan's manners were bad, eased through the doorway and stood stooping just inside with one shoulder of the shortened blue Army overcoat set solidly against the door frame.

'Just wondered how things were going,' said Homer.

'We haven't come to any agreement yet,' said Prather, 'though I hope we shall.'

'Maybe just as well you don't,' said Homer easily. 'You can probably pick up a man in Baker.'

Prather said sharply, 'If you don't mind, Homer, I will handle my own concerns.'

Lanahan flicked a look at the girl, brought his eyes back to Prather, ignoring Homer completely.

'I'd like to know a little more about this,' he said mildly. 'Like for instance, how does he,' he jerked his head at Homer without looking at him, 'fit in?'

'Mr. Flagg,' said Prather stiffly, 'is my daughter's fiancé. They are to be married shortly after we settle in the Territory. Thus, in a way, our interests are combined. Mr. Flagg will be preceding our herd with his own drive. I should like to have you handle ours.'

'By 'ours' you mean you and your daughter?'

'Yes. We are legally full partners. Since I

am not in the best of health...'

'I guess not,' said Lanahan. He stood up. 'Not a petticoat herd.'

Homer Flagg brought his shoulder off the door frame. 'I didn't think I'd have to speak to you again about that,' he said.

Lanahan took a short turning stride that brought him facing Flagg in the tight space. All the suppressed angers and frustrations of the past days came boiling, seething with the promised relief of an incipient venting. The arrogant bastard was asking for it, and whether he knew it or not, his kind rubbed Lanahan raw. 'I don't want you to open that big mouth to me again,' he said, deliberately, roughly, throwing the words full in the man's face.

Flagg's face showed shock, a whitening, and then a tiny flickering flame of violence showed inside, and his lips pulled away from his teeth in a taut grimace.

Lanahan held himself ready, waiting the first committing move, wanting it, because he was going to take the big arrogant loudmouth out and down those steps backward, with the sincere and earnest hope that he would break his neck when he hit.

Then Amos Prather made a protesting sound and came up and off the bunk to interpose his slight, bundled shape between them.

'Gentlemen,' he said sharply.

'Not me,' said Lanahan tonelessly. 'I'm no gentleman. I'll tear his head off his shoulders if he opens his mouth to me again.'

'You can try,' said Homer bleakly. He was still balanced, ready and willing.

'Homer,' said Prather, still sharply, 'you will have to excuse me. I must insist on handling my own affairs in my own way. I am sure I can do it without your help.'

Flagg smiled a tight humorless smile over the smaller man's shoulder at Lanahan. 'Don't hurry away,' he said softly.

'I won't,' promised Lanahan. The tension started to drain away then, and it left him feeling somehow tired and vague.

Prather pulled the door shut behind Homer Flagg and said a little testily, 'Sit down, Lanahan, sit down.'

'I don't think there's much more to talk about.'

Prather's lips pushed a little out and in, in an exasperated grimace. 'You haven't heard my proposition,' he said.

'All right,' said Lanahan. He moved back a step but did not sit down.

Prather seated himself with the automatic carefulness of a chronically ill man, and tipped his head back to look up at Lanahan. 'I understand a good wagon boss can deliver a herd in the Territory for a dollar a head,' said Prather. 'Frankly, I have no more than that to risk. Therefore, I want you to take full charge. Rather than a wage, I am offering you one dollar a head for my cattle, as counted at delivery. I have engaged a few hands here. You may engage as many more as you will need. I will furnish a cook wagon and team. You will furnish men and horses, and have full control over them.'

Lanahan demanded suddenly, 'How did you hear about my horses?'

He was watching closely, and he saw the two little telltale spots of color come in Prather's cheeks.

'It's no secret, is it? It's common talk that you are trailing a herd of horses into the Territory.'

'And you want the use of them to get your cattle there.'

Prather said defensively, 'Don't leap to conclusions, Mr. Lanahan. We can both gain by it. You will gain by having better broken and trained horses, which will bring a better price. You will also have the cash gain of trailing my herd, where otherwise you would have the same trip to make and the price of the horses alone.'

A small excitement was stirring inside Lanahan now, but he kept his face expressionless and his voice level.

'Sure, except I'll be half a year getting my money,' he said dryly. 'I can be halfway there before you get your cows across the Snake.'

'Except,' said Prather just as dryly, 'that

you're broke, Mr. Lanahan. You'll be lucky to get those horses to Baker City before you starve out. And I expect you'll find that expensive horse meat pretty tough to swallow.'

'Ah,' said Lanahan softly, 'now we find the peach has got a stone in it. You think you've got me straddling a split rail.'

'No, I am making you a business proposition.'

Lanahan rubbed a rough hand across the side of his jaw, the stiff beard whispering harshly against the pressure. He cut a quick look at the girl. She was pulling the fringe of her shawl carefully through her fingers, and she did not look up.

'How many head?'

'Two thousand.'

'And if I lose half of them crossing the lava, then where do we stand?'

'A good wagon boss won't lose anything like that many. If I am wrong, then I'm the one riding the—ah—split rail, I think you said.'

Inside Lanahan an outrageous desire to laugh began to grow. It was funny—the way the sight of a fat man taking a wild sprawling fall on a slick rock is funny—until you realize the man broke his back when he hit. A pair of busted flushes each trying to bluff the other; something like a con man selling a toll bridge for a gold brick...

'All right,' said Lanahan, almost without meaning to say it, 'I'll take it.'

He caught the quick lift of Prather's head, the sternly suppressed look of relief. 'Good,' said Prather. 'Good.'

'Just one thing,' said Lanahan. 'It's my job, with no advice and no strings. I hire 'em, and you feed 'em, and you advance the men their wages as they call for it, against my cut. I draw nothing till the herd is delivered. Then I get a dollar a head, less the crew's wages. Any calf increase is yours, any unbranded increase over one year old is mine. Deal?'

Prather blinked rapidly, turning the words over in his mind. He stood up and put out his hand. 'It's a deal,' he said. Lanahan took the hand, grinning inside. Prather still thought he'd conned him. For now.

'All right,' said Lanahan, 'I'll look them over in the morning. Is the gather finished here?'

'Yes,' Prather said. 'We'll pick up the rest at Baker City.'

'All right,' said Lanahan. He picked up his hat, nodded stiffly to the girl, and stepped down from the end of the wagon.

The fire had died down to a glowing bed of coals, and silent blanket-wrapped bodies encircled it where the hands had turned in. A little whirl of sparks and a lick of flames stirred as Lanahan came up, and he could see Homer Flagg hunkered down on the other side. Flagg thrust with a stick, and the dry stick caught a ball of flame on the end, to light Homer's face and steady eyes.

Lanahan rolled a smoke, squatted down and picked up a twig with a glowing end and puffed the cigarette alight. He turned away from the fire, walked out into the dark.

His horse wasn't where he'd left it. He took a short swing out and around, knowing the animal would not graze far, for it was obedient to the anchoring rein. He circled the fire completely and came back.

'Where's my horse?' he asked Flagg.

Flagg yawned widely, but his alert eyes never left Lanahan's face. 'Maybe it walked off.'

'Not that horse,' said Lanahan. He drew his pistol, thumbed back the hammer, and let it drop.

The outrageous bellow of the shot was a shocking blow on the ears. A fountain of embers leaped waist high in the fire. Flagg cursed and leaped back, slapping wildly at a coal that had fallen into the unbuttoned neck of his blue Army coat. The sleepers came up in an explosive flapping of blankets. Lanahan tipped his head back and roared, 'Nighthawk!'

A startled hail out of the dark answered him, and then a horse came pounding across the flat toward the fire.

As the rider came up, Lanahan demanded harshly, 'Is there a saddled horse out there with the cavvy?'

The man's eyes flicked briefly toward Flagg, and back again. 'I . . . I think so,' he said uncertainly. 'I . . .'

'Get him in here,' ordered Lanahan. He slid the .44 back into its holster, and moved back toward the fire.

Homer Flagg demanded roughly, 'What do you think you're pulling here?'

Clay Lanahan said flatly, almost gently, 'Don't ever touch my horse again, Flagg. And I don't want to see you in this camp tomorrow.' He turned, as the rider came up leading his horse. Lanahan did not thank the man. He took the rein, swung up, and sent a look around the fire.

The men still stood, or sat, among their blankets, carefully keeping a strict neutrality.

'Since you're all awake,' said Lanahan dryly, 'you might as well have the word. I'm roddin' this outfit. Any of you that druther not take your orders from me be gone in the morning.' He pulled the horse around and rode out.

CHAPTER THREE

Jed Martindale was still up, though it was after midnight when Lanahan rode into the camp. He looked up across the little fire and asked, 'Sell any?'

'Nope.' Lanahan swung down, unsaddled, slipped the bridle, slapped the horse on the rump and watched it make a couple of twisting crow hops out into the dark, glad to be shed of the saddle. 'Got us a job, though,' he said.

'What do we want with jobs?' Jed's voice was sardonic. 'I thought we was in the horse business.'

'Still are. Only somebody else cooks our grub and hauls our beds.' He sketched in the agreement, and Jed listened, scratching patterns with a stick on the crumbly earth the fire had dried.

'And we use the horses as cavvy, is that it? An' what do we do if them mares start droppin' foals? If that herd's cows mostly, like you say, it's goin' to be a long mean drive.'

'That's just one of the things we're bucking. You got any better ideas?'

'Not me. I reckon you're still callin' it. But how about this Prather? Think he can pay off?'

Lanahan said slowly, 'That's another sticker. But I don't see where we can get beat too bad. Prather's no cattleman. But he's sharp as a razor, otherwise. What I'll bet is, he's got this herd hocked to the horns, and if he don't move, he's bust, like us. He ain't admitting it, and I think he believes he's conned us, but the thing is, we'll have the herd. And then if he don't pay on the line, maybe we got him by the crotch with a split stick, too. And we'll be in a helluva good position to start twisting.'

'One thing I like about you, Clay,' said Jed, 'is that you're such a sweet and gentle soul.'

'Sure,' grunted Lanahan. 'I've tried that. It took me a long time to learn it, and I've got the scars to prove it. But I finally got it through my head that there ain't nobody lookin' out for me but me, and when you back into a hole, you always want to keep yourself enough leverage to get back out again. You trust somebody to hang onto you, you don't want to be surprised if he lets go.'

'You mean like a pardner, Clay?' Jed's voice was quiet, and his eyes carefully followed the squiggles the stick was making.

Lanahan reached out and cuffed Jed's hat down over his eyes. 'Not all of 'em,' he said gruffly. 'Some of 'em are so damned dumb they'll stick with a deal. They ain't very bright, but they're handy to have around.

Now I think we'd better hit the feathers. It'll be a day, tomorrow.'

He rolled into his blankets and settled himself, but his mind would not let it alone. *A sick old man, an arrogant female, and that hard-nosed—what had Prather said—fiancé? Pretty fancy, for a louse-bitten shoe stringer . . . that one and her man Homer will make a pair . . . the fire and the fur will purely fly . . .*

* * *

He kissed her, and she fought a little, but not very much, and he held her full ripe woman's body against him, hard, and kissed her again, and she liked it, and together they sank down; and then he felt a great tearing pain in his shoulder and that damned black brute stud horse had his shoulder and upper arm clamped in his vicious yellow teeth and something ripped and tore as he shook his wicked red-eyed head. He rolled and struck at the stud's head with his free fist, and then he had an iron horseshoe in his hand and he struck again, and the stud went down, and he wheeled back to the bed and groped frantically for his holster; he couldn't find it, and the girl kept hanging on, both arms around his neck, wanting him to make love to her . . . Finally he found the holster and ripped the pistol from it and threw down on the black stud and shot him through the throat, and Homer Flagg fell down and then got up, holding a hand to his bleeding throat, and reached out with a terrible groping hand and caught the wound where the stud's teeth had torn. Lanahan lashed out with the .44 which wouldn't fire, and Jed caught the flailing arm and said disgusted, 'Come on, wake up—roll out! Dammit, you gonna sleep your life away? Hell, man, you're supposed to be the early bird!'

He was awake then, but he came half out of his blankets, still half certain of threat and violence, before he caught himself.

It was still dark, but Jed had the pack horse loaded up, all but two plates of beans and bacon and bread, and the coffeepot, from which he was filling two cups.

'Come and git it,' he said, ''fore I fling it to the dickey-birds.'

Lanahan rolled out, stamped into his boots, walked over to where the big canteen hung on a limb. He tipped it with his elbow, caught the stream in his cupped hands, and flung the icy water over his face. He sputtered and scrubbed, lifted his hat to run his wet fingers through his hair, settled the hat on his head again, and considered the amenities done for the morning.

'Now,' he said. 'Let's have at 'er.'

Lanahan left the horses to Jed and rode ahead to the Prather camp, the last mile. The cook, a heavy, grouchy looking man, was stowing the last of his pots away in the chuck box at the end of the wagon. He stopped as Lanahan rode up, and demanded gruffly, 'You et yet?'

'Yes. Thanks.'

The cook scowled up at him disapprovingly. 'There's coffee left. Might as well have a cup 'fore I dump it out.'

Lanahan looked over at the Prathers' camp wagon, saw the door swing open, and said, 'Thanks, anyhow,' and rode toward the wagon.

Amos Prather came down the steep little steps slowly, bundled even heavier than he had been the night before.

'Good morning. What's first on the agenda?'

'I'll look them over,' said Lanahan. 'Run a rough tally, and move them out. Plenty of miles to go.'

Eileen Prather came out of the wagon, tipped her head back to look up at Lanahan and said, 'That was a peculiar way to call your horse, last night.'

Lanahan said gravely, 'I wasn't calling my horse, exactly. Somebody wanted to play games and I obliged them. Sorry if it bothered you.'

She looked at him steadily and carefully and said almost musingly, 'You are something of a bully, aren't you, Mr. Lanahan?'

He felt that one bring blood to his cheeks and he said shortly, 'Just bull-headed about some things, Miss Prather.' He pulled his horse around and rode away without looking back.

The four hands and the nighthawk were standing or squatting by saddled horses at a neutral distance from the wagons, being very casual in the way they rolled smokes or fiddled with rein ends. A couple stood up from their squatting position as he rode up. They looked at him, not speaking, and he knew they were judging him, with that quick merciless judgment of their breed. He said, 'I'll need your names for the tally book.' He fished a battered notebook and stub pencil out of his shirt pocket, leafed past the pages with his horse tally and a few addresses, and looked at the man on his right.

'George Bristow,' said the man. There was also Bud Armishaw, Tex Walker, Oscar Whitestaff, and the nighthawk's name was Dick Braugh. Lanahan wrote them all down, closed the book and asked, 'What are you drawing?'

'Thirty,' said George Bristow. Lanahan had already classified him as a Texas man. Double-cinched saddle, grass rope tied hard and fast to the saddle fork. The one labeled Tex, on the other hand, rode a center-fire, single-cinch saddle with dally-marks bruised deep into the leather-wrapped horn.

California or Oregon hand, thought Lanahan, which went for the nighthawk too. The other two were also Texans, as were most of the trail drovers in this country.

The Texas trails were petering out, and these were men who felt crowded by a fence twenty miles away. The Territories were opening up, and Oregon was booming with cattle. All a man had to do was trail them a thousand miles east across the sagebrush desert and lava country to the rich buffalo grass of Montana and Wyoming Territories. So the Texans drifted in from Texas and Kansas and all the byways along the west half of the country, following their trade. They brought their skill and their ready tempers, their big hats and heavy saddles, their low-slung holsters and hard-laid ropes, to work a while longer at their trade.

Thirty dollars a month, the going wage, and the day as long as it took to get the work done. No Sundays west of Omaha. Ride a half-wild horse to herd half-wild cattle, sleep and eat when you could—and broke three days after payday. Lanahan flipped the book shut and stowed it away.

He looked them over carefully. He said to the one who had spoken first, George Bristow, 'Where in the hell did you get that hat?'

The man reached up and removed the thing, a ridiculous curly brimmed derby, eyed it speculatively, and thumped it back on his head.

'You don't like my hat?' he inquired mildly. That cinched it. That nasal drawl never came from anywhere but Texas.

'Didn't say that,' said Lanahan. 'I just wondered where the hell you got it.'

'Why,' said the man, 'I bought it.' He took it off again, and stared into it, as if it might contain some wondrous secret. 'Paid three whole dollars of my hard-earned money for it. Seemed like a good idea, right then. Of course,' not quite apologetically, still looking into the empty crown, 'I was took pretty drunk at the time.' He looked up at Lanahan, eyes full of mildness and innocence. 'I had to tromp the last man didn't like it,' he added gently.

'I believe you,' said Lanahan, just as gently. 'All right. You'll draw forty a month, those of you that stick. You'll earn it. Now, I want the herd strung out and worked past here. String 'em thin so I can get some kind of a tally. Nighthawk, tell the cook to move about ten miles down-river. Let the horses go and pile in the wagon and get some shuteye, and get it now, 'cause I don't know when I'll need you again. Any questions, let's have 'em now.'

There were none. The sleep-hungry nighthawk took his horse at a walk toward the chuck wagon. Lanahan got a little handful of pebbles to help with the tally and swung back into the saddle.

Good enough hands, these. They got the herd underway without fuss or trouble, moving slowly in a long line past Lanahan. He counted ten, dropped a pebble from his right hand to his left. Ten more, and another pebble. A quarter-mile away, Jed Martindale raised his hat and held it at arm's length above his head. Lanahan waved his arm in a circle and pointed to the moving chuck wagon. Jed wagged his hat twice and swung out to turn the horse herd. Ten more—another pebble.

CHAPTER FOUR

They tallied out just under five hundred head, 497 to be exact. The two-hundred-odd steers in the bunch were about evenly divided between long yearlings and scrawny oldsters that would have to be penned and fed before they were edible, and they'd never make prime again. The she-stuff was a mixture that leaned toward Durham, but showed signs of many a miscegenation from hit-or-miss breeding with whatever range bull had been at hand.

The cavvy, which was certainly a title greater than its worth, consisted of eight horses, plus those now in service, and half of them were dog-meat plugs. Lanahan rode over to the Prathers' wagon. Someone had harnessed two horses, and now Prather was making heavy going of trying to get them hitched in.

Lanahan got down, moved the stupid acting creatures where he wanted them with authoritative voice and hands, and hooked up the tugs.

'Thank you,' said Prather. He was breathing hard, and his gloved hands were trembling. He looked pretty nearly done in. Lanahan had a sudden, almost overwhelming misgiving. He liked the looks of this thing less and less.

He said, a little more roughly than he had intended, 'You'd better keep this thing to the high ground and off of the boggy spots. You need another team, anyway.'

Prather said stiffly, 'It has done very well so far, Mr. Lanahan. I hope you found everything else to your satisfaction.'

Lanahan said bluntly, 'I did not. But I'll straighten it out. I'd advise you to saw off that miserable collection you call a cavvy to the first Hoosier you can find, and don't haggle over price. If you've got extra harness I'll see what I can dig up for a lead team, and you'd better get used to driving a four-horse hitch, because you'll never get this rig over the Blues without it. This won't be any picnic any way you look at it.'

'I suppose not,' said Prather tiredly.

Lanahan rode to catch up to the cavvy, and said, 'Jed, I'm going on ahead and roust out that poor damned nighthawk after a while and send him back here, and you pick out a couple of nags that look like they might drive and take 'em back to Prather's wagon. If he's got harness, double team it and stay there till you're sure they'll drive and he can handle 'em. Otherwise, just hitch in the fresh team. But stay with him till you're sure he's got 'em.'

'All right,' said Jed. 'Any other little chore you'd like me to take care of back there?' He leered with delicate insinuation.

Lanahan said roughly, 'Let's get one thing straight. That woman gets treated like a lady, and outside of that, she gets left strictly alone. The first sonofabitch I catch hanging around that wagon I'm goin' to beef personally unless Prather beats me to it. And that goes for all hands.'

'Even your very own pardner?' said Jed in mock astonishment.

Lanahan said wearily, 'Pop, you're thirty years too late. *I* know you're just as safe as if you were gelded, but I don't want you setting a bad example for the *young* men.'

'Will you kindly,' said Jed with dignity, 'get the hell out of here?'

Lanahan grinned wider, touched his hat in

mock salute and rode on.

The cook rode the high seat of the chuck wagon, his arms extended, shifting to the sawing disparate pull of reins from the four-horse hitch. He looked around grouchily as Lanahan rode alongside.

Lanahan said, 'That team going to make it all right?' Then: 'What do I call you?'

The cook said grumpily, 'You don't call me Mr. Longquist. And they'll make it, or there won't be any hide left on their butts. Most people call me Eben. You want I should feed them straight-gut hands for noon or not?'

'Wanted to talk to you about that, Eben. If you'll haul in and throw out some hot grub for the hands for a nooning. I want to push this herd till plumb dark. I want 'em tired and ready to bed. I expect the hands will take what they can get before they hit their blankets.'

Eben said in an outraged tone, 'You tryin' to insult me, Ramrod? B'God, you say so, they git hot chuck at dinner an' they git it at supper too. Man's workin' he's got to eat. Just don't come cryin' about the cost of the grub-pile, thass all.'

For a moment Lanahan eyed him speculatively, considering cutting him to size, and then, knowing that a decent cook was a pearl without price, said, 'If you can swing it, I'll appreciate it.'

‘Yeah, and soon’s you git the wrinkles out o’ yer belly, you’ll be growlin’ an’ bitchin’ like the rest of ’em. Just remember I only got two hands, thass all.’

There was snow in the Blue Mountains—wet, melting snow. They got an overnight flurry, on their first mountain camp, and it was wet and cold too, half slush, which was nearly melted away by mid morning. This was Oregon Trail country, and some forty years of emigration had hacked a plenitude of roadways, and nearly two generations of wagon-train night fires had thinned the timber, but cows in timber can move the saintliest of men to prayerful profanity. These were not saintly men. Their blue-rimmed, purple-tinted profanity echoed and ricocheted and volleyed through the stolid unheeding pines. the half-broke horses didn’t like the brush or the riders, the cows didn’t like the brush or the horses or the riders, and the riders hated the cows, the brush, the horses and themselves with an intensity that can come to man when he is cold and wet and hard-worked and knowing that the moment he relaxes he’s likely to get pitched tail over tin cup halfway down a mountainside by a half-wild horse just waiting the chance.

Lanahan pushed them hard—men and animals—and drove himself as mercilessly as any. It was mean work, and tough titty for breakfast, but that was the story of any cowhand's life. There's only one way to git to Baker City, and that's over the goddam mountains ... *Heya-a-ah! Git along, there!*

* * *

Baker City was booming. She had brick buildings and wood buildings, and tin-covered buildings with the tin stamped in block shapes painted red to resemble brick. Every last one was jammed full so that a large block of the town was housed in tents and canvas-covered wood frames. Hobnailed miner's boots, tramping the board sidewalks. Granger wagons, canvas-covered; high-sided ore wagons, groaning and grumbling behind twelve-horse jerk-line teams. Cowponies standing hipshot at the solid lines of hitching racks, slow freighters, bounding Concords dust-coated and rattling, ending their long haul from railhead at Kelton, Utah.

Wide-brimmed hats and Texas drawls. Hard derbies and Midwest twangs. Chinese, with pigtails coiled neatly under stiff black hats with the brims turned up all around and the crowns smooth and undented, just as they came off the counter. Traveling in little knots and clusters, the almond-eyed Orientals clutched their valises and cloth-wrapped bundles fearfully close, knowing that a China boy was of little value here, and one never knew when these brawling white brothers might feel an urge to entertainment.

Baker City, Oregon, Year of Our Lord 1883, roaring and brawling and stamping her iron-shod feet, ingesting worthless looking ore, spewing out wealth in bricks and ingots of gold; chewing with giant teeth at the forest to make the rough boards that went onto the frame so fast that they were still wet with sap, and the sun twisted and warped them with leverage enough to pull nails. Baker City, the jump-off for the Territories, last chance to buy a sturdy wagon or a saddle, to fill the grub box or shoe a horse.

A last roaring night for the drovers, last chance for a drink and a listen to the tinny pianos in the joints that never closed their doors, but racketed the full clock around. Herds grazing off the grass for miles around; herds of two thousand, four thousand, ten thousand; sons and daughters of the family cows that had plodded three thousand miles across the nation behind a covered wagon in years past. That was Baker City. Rough and tough and rich. And proud of it.

Lanahan left the herd ten miles out, and rode into the town. He threaded through traffic until he spotted a busy saloon, swung down, and entered the place. He spotted two men, riders unmistakable, idling at the bar end, and he stepped up alongside and lifted a hand to the bar man.

He was served, and he turned half toward the pair and said, 'Would either one of you be on the market for a riding chore?'

The nearest one turned just as slightly, gave Lanahan a casual survey and said amiably, 'Could be. What's the deal?'

'Trailing east. Mixed herd. Top pay for a good man.'

'What's the outfit?'

'Prather outfit. Just pulled in.'

'That's the AP Connected brand? Cow outfit?'

'That's right.'

His man said still amiably. 'Well, hell, I still got jingle money in my pocket. Reckon not today, mister.'

Lanahan shrugged slightly. 'Your privilege. Top wages, though, and a good cook.'

'Sure, provided we collect.'

'What's that mean?' He kept his full attention on the man, seeing that first amiability fade.

The man said coolly and detachedly, 'No offense. I'm still stakey, is all. Ain't took in all the town yet. That right, Clint?'

His companion said with forced humor. 'That's about it. Still jinglin' and ain't seed the elephant yet. Maybe some other time, mister.'

'Yeah, sure,' said Lanahan carefully. He paid for his drink and left the place.

He went down the street. He said nothing on entering the next place but found himself a spot where he could lean a shoulder against a wall and roll a smoke and listen. He heard little that he did not already know; a man could hire out almost at will, with a choice of half a dozen outfits; that every bovine critter capable of walking or staggering seemed to be funneled through Baker City for drives, long or short, eastward; that the cattle outfits were hiring, the mines were hiring, the freighters and packers and builders were hiring; and a damn good thing too, while she lasts. Remember Abilene, ten-twelve years back, when Wild Bill was roddin''er, and Dodge—now there was one with the hair on ... Lanahan pushed himself away from the wall and went in search of Amos Prather.

He saw Homer Flagg first: Flagg dismounted and holding the reins in his hands, talking to a group of four men, apparently his own riders, for he spoke with an authoritative gesturing and got little reply from his listeners. Flagg saw Lanahan, gave him a look of recognition and then as Lanahan came on to pass, turned away from his listeners and gave Lanahan his full attention.

'Lanahan,' said Flagg suddenly. He pulled

his horse around behind him, leading it by the reins, stepped out and away from the board walk. 'Can a man talk to you without having to fight about it, Lanahan?'

Lanahan pulled up, swinging his mount slightly toward Flagg. 'Depends on the man, and what he wants to talk about,' he said in a neutral voice.

'This is strictly business.'

'What is it?'

'Maybe we can find a more private place to talk than this.' Flagg was holding his rein chest high, slapping the end against his other palm.

'I don't know any business we've got that's that damned private.' He didn't like the man, and made no effort to hide it, and his tone brought a faint change in Flagg's high color.

'All right. You want to sell those horses of yours?'

'Eventually. At Wyoming prices.'

'This isn't Wyoming, man.'

'Now that I know. Probably a hundred men around here could have told you that, if you'd asked.'

Flagg whipped the rein end hard against his own boot top, an explosive sound that made his horse flinch backward. 'You make it hard on a man, don't you, Lanahan?'

'You're dealin'. Let's see 'em, or forget it.'

'I'll buy your horses. The whole outfit, if

you'll set a reasonable price.'

Lanahan probed at the man, trying to read him, discover his feelings and his motives, and saw only the watchful and heavy face that Flagg showed to the world. Flagg's eyes were steadily on his, showing nothing, no discomfiture at this close, evaluating scrutiny. Lanahan said finally, 'See me in Wyoming, then.'

'I don't think so. You'll be lucky to make it past the Snake. No, the deal is now or never. I'm not going to haggle with you.'

'Don't then,' said Lanahan. He neck-reined his mount slightly left, started to move on.

'Better think it over,' said Flagg. 'You're pouring sand down a rat hole. The word's all over town that you'll likely never even move that shoestring outfit off the bed ground.'

'So it is,' said Lanahan softly. 'And maybe one day I'll find where it started. And when I do, maybe I'll drag that man down Front Street by the feet so the whole town can see what a sneaking liar looks like. Meantime, don't go to sleep in front of that shoestring outfit. You might get walked right into the ground.'

Flagg kept a close and watchful attention on him. 'What does that mean?' he said. 'Are you threatening something, or just spitting into the wind?'

'Suppose you figure it out,' said Lanahan.

He touched his mount with the rowels and rode on without looking back. And wished he was as confident as he'd sounded.

He found Prather coming out of the livery stable up street from the Western Hotel. Prather looked sick and worried. 'We'll be taking delivery on the rest of the cattle shortly,' said Prather. 'Did you hire any more men?'

'I did not. And I doubt I will, with the talk that's going around. So if I'm going to be the last one to know it, I'd like a straight answer. Just how close to broke is this outfit, anyway?'

Prather stared at him, and slowly his eyes turned cold and expressionless. His narrow shoulders straightened. 'Come with me, young man,' he snapped, and with the first show of energy Lanahan had seen in him, he turned and strode away, without waiting to see whether Lanahan followed. He strode at a rapid gait to the corner, turned, walked to the third doorway and turned in without breaking stride. Lanahan was forced to hurry, to tie his horse and follow.

Within the bank lobby, he caught up as Prather stopped at a low railing and spoke to the man just inside at a cluttered desk.

'Why, good day again, Mr. Prather,' said the man.

'Good day,' said Mr. Prather tonelessly. 'I want only to ask you one question, in this young man's presence, if I may. If I were to write an order on this bank at this moment for ten thousand dollars, would you honor it?' He made the 'young man' sound like a sneer, and the complete question entirely scornful.

The man behind the desk flicked his watchful eyes to and fro between them, and then with an air of faint amusement said, 'Of course, Mr. Prather. Will you want it in gold or greenbacks?'

'Neither, thank you. The answer was not for my ears. I am sorry if I have imposed on your time. Thank you again, and good day.' He wheeled, still without looking at Lanahan, and strode away. Lanahan followed, feeling like a fool, and itchingly aware of the banker's amused eyes on his back. He found Prather at the hitching rack, standing, looking neither right nor left.

'All right,' said Lanahan. 'I had my foot in it, clear up to my knee. I suppose now you'll be needing another wagon boss.'

Prather's shoulders slowly lost their rigid set. He turned slowly to face Lanahan. 'No,' he said, finally. 'No, I think I'll go along with the one I've got. I expect he'll be a good and conscientious man, if he ever learns not to try and outsmart himself. Your suspicions over-ride your wisdom sometimes, young man.'

'Reckon that's the way I am. You want to

get yourself another man, there's no hard feelings. I asked for it.'

'If I wanted another man, I would be looking for him this minute. I hired you to handle my herd. Handle it.'

'Yes, sir,' said Lanahan, who hadn't said sir to any man since his father, who had insisted on it. He ducked under the tie rail and got his horse and swung up. In the saddle, he felt a little less like a scolded ten-year-old, and he looked back at Prather and said, 'If the smell of some of that money got around town it might change some of the talk.'

'We'll make out,' said Prather. Then he tipped his head back and smiled. It was a thin smile, with still a touch of frostiness about it, but it was a smile. 'We'll make out,' he repeated.

Lanahan rode back to his herd. He put his mind to the multitude of things that needed doing before he could put the herd on the trail.

CHAPTER FIVE

Lanahan walked his horse through the slow surge of traffic that filled the street from walk to walk. His shirt was open at the throat, and dust lay in the folds of his neckerchief. May second, a full month since he had taken the herd at the Grande Ronde. Nearly two weeks to trail to Baker City. Two weeks of marking time waiting for the rest of the herd.

He swung down, looped a rein on the hitching rail and ducked under, feeling the little giddiness of tiredness all through him. He hadn't averaged four hour's sleep a night since he'd taken the rest of the herd. Five men were spread too thin to hold two thousand head of strange cattle who had to be close-herded when a dozen other herds were within shooting distance. And still nobody seemed to want to work a cow herd. Most especially the Prather herd.

The Silver Dollar was jammed, even now, before noon. Three bar men hustled, pouring, making change. Lanahan worked in to the bar, got a drink without even asking for it, and stopped the busy bar man long enough to ask the question he was getting sick of asking, 'Know anybody that wants a riding chore?'

The man rattled change on the bar, waved an arm at the crowded room and said shortly, 'Take your pick. Looks like a hundred riders there.' He hurried off down the bar.

Then someone said right at Lanahan's elbow, 'Are you hirin' mister?'

The kid couldn't have been much more than sixteen, though he was as tall as

Lanahan. His arms dangled at his sides, much bone and little muscle, ending in knobby-knuckled hands that were thrust inches past outgrown sleeves. His lips were full, childish almost, and a little uncertain twitch showed on them under Lanahan's close inspection.

Lanahan said, 'Sorry, kid. I've already got a horse wrangler.'

The boy's lips twitched again. 'It don't have to be wrangler does it?' he asked. 'Reckon I can do my part, an' I'm willing to work short wages to...'

'Look,' said Lanahan almost roughly, 'nobody works for me for short wages. If he's not worth full pay he's not worth anything. But I need top hands because I'm running a short crew.'

He took another quick look at the boy's face and said more gently, 'Look, kid, you'll probably get the same answer from any of the trail outfits, unless they need an extra horse wrangler or some such. Best bet for you is to get in on one of the holding crews, or a branding job. If you keep your eyes open and your mouth shut you can learn a lot, and maybe next year you can hook on some place.'

The boy said stiffly, 'Thanks,' and wheeled away, walking stiff-backed and hurriedly, as if he were going some place definite. But once outside the door, he paused, looking uncertainly up and down the crowded walks. Lanahan tossed off his drink and walked over to the gambling tables.

The roulette table was getting a big play. They were banked around it three deep, and Lanahan sidled through until he could see over another man's shoulder. Directly across from the croupier was a rider, a narrow-shouldered whip of a man, hat pushed back on his head, yellowish, hawklike eyes fixed intently on the little white ball as it bounded about the wheel. He had a tremendous stack of chips before him, and one narrow hand restlessly picked up a small stack, dribbled them back, picked them up, let them chink and whisper again. The ball clattered, slowed, hit a slot, bounded, clicked, bounced again, caught in a slot and rode around the wheel.

'Black,' said the croupier. He pushed a stack across to match the one before the rider, and then Lanahan saw that the whole pile had been on that color.

'Let 'er ride,' said the rider.

The croupier looked up sharply. 'All of it?'

'The tail with the hide. Spin 'er.'

The wheel whirred. The little ivory ball spun around the dished rim, opposing the motion of the wheel. It lost its speed, and began to drift down toward the numbered slots, and the crowd began to press in, a physical leaning to get closer, to see. The rider's hawk face showed nothing but a faint compression at the corners of his thin lips.

The ball bounded crazily. Twice, it seemed it had caught, and twice it dribbled out to click again on the walls of the little slots. Then it caught and rode.

A windy sigh came out of the group, a mass exhalation that seemed almost on cue.

'Red,' said the croupier. He reached out with his little rake and dragged the double pile toward him. Lanahan estimated quickly that there must be nearly five thousand dollars in the stack. The rider looked at the wheel. His lips curved upward at the corners in a wry smile.

'You're as bad as a woman,' he told the wheel, and then he turned carelessly away. 'Who's goin' to buy me a drink? That spin broke me.'

The croupier showed his narrow, professional smile and slid a ten-dollar chip back across the board. 'Can't let a real sport go broke in the Silver Dollar,' he said.

'Nor muzzle the ox which treadeth the grain,' murmured the rider. 'Thanks.'

Lanahan moved in at the man's elbow as he got his drink.

'Interested in a job?' he said.

His man said without looking around, 'Hell, I got money left.'

Lanahan retorted easily, 'I've walked far enough for one day, and you're a gambler.

Flip me for it. Then you're either broke and got a job, or you're flush with twenty.'

The chip was blue, with yellow figures on it; a dollar sign on the back, a woman's helmeted head on the other, labeled Lady Luck.

'Call it,' said the man. He flipped the chip spinning in the air. 'Heads,' said Lanahan.

The chip hit the bar, bounced, flipped over. Heads.

The rider shrugged, said, 'Hello, boss.' He turned his yellow hawk eyes full on Lanahan for the first time, looking him over carefully. 'Where we goin'?' he asked.

'Wyoming Territory. Bighorn country.'

'Big herd?'

'Two thousand. Cows, mostly.'

The man grunted. 'Now you *will* have to buy me a drink,' he said. Lanahan signaled the bar man. Then he got out his tally book.

'What's the name?'

The man took his drink, set the glass down carefully. 'Tennessee,' he said.

'Tennessee what?'

'Just Tennessee.' It was quiet, but it was definite, and Lanahan shrugged and wrote it down. 'Forty a month,' he said, and looked full into the yellow eyes. 'And I don't want any sheriff trouble around the camp.'

For just a moment, Tennessee's eyes were hard and sharp, and then he said lightly, 'I ain't lost no sheriffs.'

'Good enough,' said Lanahan. 'If you're here in an hour, I'll ride out with you. Or you can ask for the Prather outfit.'

'I'll be here.'

That was blind luck. Lanahan cruised the joints for another hour, and got solid resistance. Either they were already working, or were so stakey they wouldn't talk business riding with a cow herd. He turned back to the Silver Dollar.

He saw Tennessee, still at the bar, showing no other reaction to his drinking than a slightly heightened color, and then he spotted the kid who had hit him for a job, standing idly, a little uncertainly, at a rear table watching a poker game. For an instant, he rejected the thought and then he shrugged and tramped down the long room.

He came up behind the boy and asked, 'Land that job yet?'

The boy turned, recognized him, said stiffly, 'No.'

'Still want to ride for me?'

The kid's face paled, flushed violently. His lips quivered, and he blurted out, 'Hell yes. Sure.'

Lanahan said shortly, 'No use stringing you, kid. I aim to get a day's work out of you, every day, all the way. So I'll tell you right now. If you can't cut it, I'm going to fire you, quick. I'm not expecting you to be a top hand, but you'd better smarten up fast, or not at all. You'll draw forty a month. What's your name?'

The kid swallowed, hugely. His full lips worked hard at shaping the words. 'Jim. Jim Riordan. And thanks, mister, thanks.' Then his big, bony hands came up, and the right hand cracked the knuckles of the left in an agony of embarrassment. 'Only ... only I ain't got a horse, mister. I...'

'Wouldn't do you any good if you did, kid. Nobody rides his private horse for me. There'll be a wagon loading grub at that store on the corner of Front and Broadway this afternoon. AP Connected. Get your plunder together and ride out with it.'

'Sure,' said the boy. 'Sure. And thanks.'

Lanahan put his hand on Tennessee's elbow and asked, 'Ready?'

'Any time.' He shoved the jumble of change that was left from the ten-dollar chip toward Lanahan, who said, 'Save it for tobacco. It's a long trip.'

Tennessee pocketed the change without looking at it and they walked out together. Tennessee was riding an unbranded buckskin, a snuffy little beast, and before he stepped up, Tennessee tucked the coiled end of the *mecate*, the light picket line, under his belt in an unconscious gesture. Lanahan saw it, and marked it without comment.

A lot of desert riders got that habit. So did the ones who rode the lonely trails and expected to be shot at. Even if a man were knocked, or thrown, out of the saddle, that coiled line paid out slowly enough for a man to make a grab to escape being left afoot.

They worked their way through the shouldering traffic, and Lanahan jerked a thumb at Tennessee's coiled catch rope.

'You'll have a chance to stretch the kinks out of that tomorrow.'

'So?'

'Fifteen hundred of them to stretch and throw and run a brand on before we can move out.'

'No corrals or chutes?'

'They're all full from hell to breakfast. Besides, they cost money. We'll do it the hard way. Rope 'em and bust 'em, and you'll sweat for your forty and found.'

'I just knew this wasn't my day. Why did you have to catch me broke?' He rode easily, this Tennessee, straight-backed and long-legged, watching his surroundings casually. But Lanahan had the feeling that this man was completely aware of everything that moved within his sight.

A fence-jumper, Lanahan thought. *Hope he keeps out of trouble till we're done with this.*

He pulled up at the chuck wagon and swung down. Eben Longquist, the cook, came around the far side to demand crossly, 'You et yet?' Eben's face was formidably grouchy, but Lanahan was used to that now.

Eben never had a kind word for anybody, but he hated the sight of a hungry man. the coffeepot was always on the fire, every minute the wagon was not in motion, and no rider showed at the wagon without hearing the grumpy demand, 'You et yet?'

'Thanks, Ebe,' said Lanahan, 'I could stand a cup of coffee. This is Tennessee. He's riding for the outfit.'

Ebe growled angrily. 'Glad to know yuh,' and produced two tin cups. 'You want it sweet or straight?' he demanded truculently of Tennessee.

Tennessee shrugged. 'Straight's fine.'

Ebe glared at him. 'Take a little sweetenin',' he growled, 'we got lots of it.'

'I like it black and straight,' said Tennessee. He cut an inquiring eye at Lanahan.

'All right,' said Eben ungraciously. 'It's your stummick.'

'Ebe, here,' explained Lanahan straight-faced, 'was put out, a while back. One of the boys went over a cutbank chasin' a wild one and broke his neck. Wouldn't eat supper that night, and it hurt Eben's feelings. I don't think he really forgave that man till we buried him.'

Tennessee chuckled, and Ebe said roughly, 'Well, if you got what you want, I got work to do.' He stamped around the side of the wagon and made a great indignant clattering of pans.

Then Lanahan became aware of Tennessee. He was holding the steaming tin cup level with his chin, but he was looking over it at the Prather wagon, some fifty yards away. Eileen came down the steps to shake out a small rug in the breeze.

Her sleeves were rolled above her elbows and she had undone the three top buttons of her tight bodice against the day's heat, and the sun made a little nimbus of reflected light about her rich chestnut hair. The little breeze pressed her dress familiarly to her body.

Tennessee said quietly, but with a touch of velvet in his voice, 'I think maybe I'll like this job after all.'

Lanahan said shortly, 'Maybe not. She owns this outfit, and besides, she's spoken for.'

The man's curiously yellow eyes came hard on Lanahan across the rim of the cup. 'Some things change,' he said gently. 'I had five thousand dollars in my hands a couple hours ago, but I ain't got 'em now. Things change.'

'Maybe,' grunted Lanahan, 'but I doubt it this time. She needs gentling maybe, but I doubt you'll be the man to do it.'

'You wouldn't care to wager, would you?' murmured Tennessee. A devilish grin split his hawk face, white even teeth flashing in the sun. For the first time, Lanahan saw that Tennessee was a handsome man.

'Forget it,' said Lanahan, almost roughly.

Tennessee's sardonic grin flashed again. 'I just work for you, Lanahan,' he said softly. 'You don't own me.'

'No,' agreed Lanahan, 'but I'm roddin' this outfit, and don't you forget that.'

CHAPTER SIX

Lanahan scrubbed a forearm across his face and blinked red eyes which felt as if they were full of sand. Tennessee cut a cow out of the herd, crowded her away, and Lanahan moved in from behind. The cow bawled and broke into a lumbering trot, while they boxed her and kept her headed. Lanahan whipped a small loop ahead, dropped it over her horns. Tennessee waited until they were within a few yards of the fire and the cow was starting to veer off, then flipped his rope low and hissing to snare her hind feet. He wheeled his pony aside, and the cow, her hind legs snatched from under her, went down on one ham, and then a braced foreleg buckled as George Bristow ran down Lanahan's rope to dump her and sit on her head.

Oscar Whitestaff brought the smoking

iron, his hands muffled in two clumsy pads of gunny sacking, braced one foot on her heaving ribs, set the iron, not roughly, but firmly. A spurt of white stinking smoke rolled up from the scorching iron, and the cow bawled and kicked convulsively, her round eyes rolling frantically. Oscar trotted back to the fire.

Lanahan slacked his rope and George flipped the loop off the cow's horns. Lanahan reefed in his rope, a long arm's reach to the coil, giving it that last shrewd twist of his fingers that laid the coil in his left hand, rode closer as George snatched Tennessee's heel rope loose.

The cow came lurching to her feet, hooking wildly from side to side, and George dodged. Lanahan rode at the cow, sheltering George behind him, and Tennessee moved in from the side with a shrill rebel yell. Together they hazed the cow toward the already branded cut that young Jim Riordan was holding, and as Jim came in to take over, Lanahan and Tennessee wheeled back to cut out another unbranded animal.

Tex Walker and Bud Armishaw came in toward the fire in their turn, the cow at a lumbering gallop. Bud with his rope already on her horns. Tex made his heelcast, missed, and cursed automatically. Bud spurred ahead, flipped the long bight of his rope over the cow's back and swung his horse sharply to the side. The galloping cow hit the end of the rope. Her head was yanked around, the tautening rope snatched her hind legs from under her, and her rump went high in the air as she crashed down, hard.

Lanahan pulled his horse up alongside Bud and said sharply, 'Don't make me tell you again, Bud. You're not busting range steers. These are bred cows. Take it easy.'

Bud said hotly, 'Get me a heeler that can handle a rope, then.'

Lanahan saw the temper in the man, the ready irritability of a man hard-worked and hot, and he said easily, 'We all miss one once in a while. Keep your shirt on,' He looked over at Tennessee, jerked his head slightly toward Bud, and then called, 'Tex, let's you and me take a couple. Tennessee's too fast for me.'

Tex said tightly, 'Look, if you ain't happy...'

'Sure I'm happy,' said Lanahan roughly. 'I'm so damned happy I feel like kissing every cow in the herd. Now pick out a nice fat slow one. My pistol pockets need a rest.

It worked. Tex grinned gibingly and snorted, 'What's the matter, pappy? Gettin' old?' He did not miss a cast the rest of the day.

Eileen Prather rode with her father part way, and continued on across the valley when he turned off to Baker City. He was not a good rider, and looked out of place on a horse. Despite the warmth of the day and the scarf that covered his neck and chest under his buttoned coat, he was not warm, and she saw his shoulders shake with his coughing as he rode away from her. She thought, *He's wrapped up too much in this thing. He should be resting with nothing to worry him.*

The injustice of her rebellious thought was plain as soon as she used it. Her father was doing what he thought he must do; and since he could not keep his store in Portland and live, he must do something else. Now, with his every dollar tied up in this cattle herd, he was committed. It was too late to retrace his steps. *He'll be better anyway, on the high plains*, she thought. *It was the dampness and the rain that hurt him, in Portland. If the winters are bad, he can leave the ranch in a manager's hands and follow the sun. We can . . .*

The thought that interrupted puzzled her. She was not a particularly introspective woman. But the intruding thought was just a bit of a jar. *But it won't be 'we.' It won't be that way after I'm married to Homer . . . 'We' will be Homer and I . . .* The thought brought a stillness to her face, not an uncertainty but a straightforward thoughtfulness that showed in eyes slightly narrowed, lips unconsciously pouted just a trifle, so that a little hollow came under her smooth sun-browned cheeks.

Only it wasn't working that way, exactly. Her thoughts circled warily, stealthily, treading delicately, as a cat treads at sight of a new and unexplained motion. String, it knows. But this string does not lie limp and quiet. It twitches and creeps, and instinct says, 'Leap.' Caution says, 'Wait—investigate.'

So Eileen's thoughts walked tiptoe about the thread, and when she looked closely the thread was a snarl, for Homer was there—and so was the black-bearded ruffian Clay Lanahan—and Eileen felt a flush coming under the smooth tan of her cheeks. She blinked rapidly and told herself sharply to quit woolgathering. She put her mind to it—and could not force the two faces apart. It was infuriating. What kind of a woman would look twice at that roughnecked, bullying unshaven boor?

Only one as bad as himself, came the instant comforting thought, and she nodded triumphantly.

She imagined him kissing a woman—one of those painted hussies she'd seen in Baker City—and she noticed indignantly that he seemed to be enjoying it. Her mind delicately drew back, and walked away tiptoe—but kept looking back over one shoulder. The pony shied indignantly under her at the totally unexpected bite of her quirt. She was kept busy for a moment to keep her seat on the sidesaddle, and her full riding skirt was whipped a little higher than decorum would permit, even if there was not another soul in sight. She sniffed and straightened her back.

The way-station came in sight, a square shack that crowded the corrals at the back, where a change of horses was kept for the Kelton-Boise-Baker City stage. Homer was already there, and he came outside as she rode up and put his arms up to help her down. She was still half-angry with the confusion of her thinking, and she kissed him a little more warmly than she had intended.

Instantly she felt his strength. His hands left their helping grip on her arms and went around her, and he pulled her hard against him and again kissed her. 'Sweet Eileen,' he murmured.

She moved back quickly, made totally unnecessary brushing motions at her full riding skirt, keeping her eyes intently down until she felt a little of the flush leaving her face.

She looked up to see Homer's eyes on her, careful and considering, and he said low-voiced, 'It will be a long trip, Eileen. I guess we'll have to say good-by this time. I'm making a long drive tomorrow, and we should hit the Snake the day after.' His eyes seemed to be cataloguing her face, feature by feature, almost hungrily. 'I hate to think I'll have to wait four months to see you again,' he said.

Again, the feeling of unease came on her—and she had never felt so with Homer before. He was tall and broad, wide of chin, and in ten or fifteen years he would be heavy. Not soft. He worked too hard for that. But there were no angles to him now, for his strength showed in every part of his body; the thick shoulders that crowded his wool shirt, the muscular column of his neck above the loosely knotted bandanna, the wide, capable hard-worked hands that were a little rough and battered from the weather and the rope.

He was like that in his thinking too, she knew. Not stolid, but direct, hardened a bit by his experience, with the bluntness of a man who has made his own chances as he went; not driven or harried but ambitious and knowing that what a man wants does not always fall into his lap from simple want. He went after his desires with hard work, and he wanted her. That much was plain to see as he stood before her now.

He said almost musingly, 'It's a long time to wait, Eileen. I'll be driving past Boise. Why couldn't we be married there?'

She shook her head almost automatically, while a tiny thread of doubt ran through her.

Because the same thought had occurred to her, and she wondered now why she rejected it so quickly.

'No, Homer,' she said gently. 'You know how it is. I must stay with Father until we are settled. Then we'll be able to think of ourselves.'

His face was almost somber, so quiet and still was his expression for a moment. He pulled off his hat and ran his fingers through his thick, curling blond hair. He said gustily, 'I'm not so sure it's so necessary, this drive of your father's. He has saddled himself with poor, cheap animals, when he could have come in with me; bought good steers for a sure quick turnover; he could have set himself up well, with the one drive.'

She said, 'You know he wouldn't, Homer. That would be like riding your coat tails, and Dad isn't like that. He must make his own way, in whatever he does. Besides, he wants stock to build on—brood stock.' She smiled faintly. 'He can be a stubborn man, you know, and I'm not sure he is wrong in this.'

'Well, then, I guess it can't be helped.' Then with a closer attention, 'How is your wagon boss working out?'

For some reason, she felt a trifle flustered. 'Mr. Lanahan? Well, he is a highhanded man, though he seems to know his business. The men seem to get along pretty well with him; but then, I suppose they must—I don't think he'd hesitate to discharge any one of them who didn't follow his orders. Sometimes he seems hard on them, but he doesn't seem to spare himself either. But then, what can we do but make the best of him now?'

'It's never too late to change,' said Homer bluntly. 'He'd not last out the first day, working for me.'

She tried to keep herself from questioning his reasoning, not disloyally, but from true interest, knew she could not question in any event, and said merely, 'We haven't much choice, Homer. We need him, we need his horses. Just for this little while,' smiling as she spoke.

He returned her smile, but again he breathed gustily, almost sighing, 'You're right, of course. But I'm in love with you, and that makes a man selfish. Don't make me wait too long.' He reached out again, brought her to him, and kissed her. Then he stepped back, looking at her broodingly with deepset blue eyes and said in an unsatisfied voice, 'I guess this is good-by, Eileen. It's thirty miles back to my herd. Forty, by tonight.'

Eileen said quickly and compassionately, 'Homer, I'm not trying to keep you dangling. I just can't do any differently.'

Homer smiled suddenly and widely. 'Of course,' he said. 'But you can't blame me for being just a little impatient.'

He picked her up effortlessly, kissed her quickly as her face came level with his, and set her in her saddle in one easy motion. 'I'll be counting the days,' he said.

She gave him a smile. She found the stirrup with her left foot, lifted her right knee over the hooklike horn of the sidesaddle and arranged her skirt. 'Good-by, Homer.'

He watched her ride out, and then as she looked back, she saw him stepping into his own saddle. He turned to wave his hat to her, and she raised a hand in reply.

* * *

Lanahan took the branding iron at noon, put the kid, Jim Riordan, at George Bristow's place of wrestling them down, brought Jed in from the horse herd. Only Tennessee and Bud stayed with the roping chore.

Jim came to grief almost immediately. The first critter was brought in and heeled, and the boy ran down the rope, flung himself against the cow's shoulders to flatten her. The cow made a scrambling pull with her braced forelegs and whipped her head fretfully against the taut horn rope. The rounded side of one up-curving horn struck the lad across the face, and he staggered back and the blood began to well from his abused nose.

Bud Armishaw yelled sarcastically, 'Do it again. Muh brudder didn't see it.' Lanahan dropped the heated iron and ran out. He hooked an elbow under the cow's muzzle, grabbed a horn, and twisted her head as he kicked behind a knee to make the braced joint bend. The leg folded, and the cow lay flat, stretched between the two ropes.

'You all right, kid?'

The boy's hand was cupped over the lower part of his face, and two unconscious tears of pain streaked the dirt of his cheeks, but he said gruffly, 'Sure.' He wiped at his dripping nose with his shirt sleeve and spread a gory streak across his face, but he moved in to throw his weight clumsily into holding the cow's head down.

Lanahan stamped the branding iron, the smoke rose, and he delayed returning to the fire to watch while the kid loosed the ropes.

'Heel rope last,' said Lanahan sharply.

The kid looked at him uncertainly and said, 'George...'

'George is an old hand and knows his own way best. You do like I tell you. Turn her head loose, while Tennessee keeps a strain on the heel rope. When you take the rope off her horns, keep a hand on her nose so you can hold her till you get your feet under you. Then get out of the way so the heeler can let her go.'

Young Jim followed directions. He

loosened the loop over her horns as Bud gave him slack, and the cow lurched under him. The kid frantically flung his weight on the cow's neck, held it down with one knee, and fumbled the rope again.

'Cripes,' said Bud, not loudly, but clearly, 'that damned kid don't know beans.' The kid flushed painfully, savagely ripped the rope free, and tossed the limp loop aside without looking at Bud. Tennessee shook his heel rope loose and let the cow up, and as she started to wheel on him, Jim Riordan snatched off his hat and slapped her across the face. The cow made a bucking leap, lashed out with her heels like a kicking horse, and then Tennessee was crowding her out, and Oscar Whitestaff and Jed Martindale hazed another in toward the fire.

Lanahan thrust the used iron into the fire, and readied another, working on the hot iron handles with a wadded gunnysack in each hand. The kid roughed at his nose again with his sleeve.

'Don't let it throw you,' said Lanahan for the boy's ears alone. Jim gave him a quick offended look and set his chin. He had hold of Jed's head rope and was running down it to the cow almost before Oscar could dump her with the heel rope. He was clumsy, but he did not spare himself. Lanahan said no more to him.

The work was a dirty, tiring grind. Dust

and stinking smoke and scorching iron. Mouth filled with cotton, and gritting sand between the teeth. Noise and heat and work that drove pain deep into a man's bones.

The kid was staggering by mid-afternoon, but he made no complaint. He grinned a stiff grin of tiredness, and his knees shook as he stood during the precious few seconds of waiting for another critter, but he flung himself doggedly and clumsily onto every one as it came in, and lay panting while Lanahan applied the iron.

Jed Martindale rode close to Lanahan, and without looking at him as he coiled his rope, said quietly, 'That lad's about tuckered out. Want I should spell him?'

Lanahan blinked red-rimmed eyes at him. 'He's drawing a man's pay,' he said roughly.

'Yeah, but...'

'But nothing. If he can't cut it, he can quit.'

Jed shrugged, and moved away. Lanahan branded the next one, dropped the iron back into the fire, and said, 'Take a breather, huh?' He tramped back away from the fire, pulled away the flour sack covering the water bucket, and drank a dipperful. He handed the dipper to the kid and started rolling a smoke, watching the boy over the work his fingers were doing.

The ropers came in, swung down and had a drink, not making a point of it, but all taking a quick look at the boy before they swung back into their saddles.

'All right,' said Lanahan. He dropped his half-smoked cigarette and scuffed it out with his boot. 'Let's hit it again.'

The afternoon wore on, in a grinding monotony. Run, scramble, fight. Hissing of iron, whisper of rope, bawling of cows. The boy was hanging on by nerve alone, now.

A tough, stringy steer came in to the fire, a scarred beast branded on both sides, brands that had to be vented by drawing a single line through them with the edge of the iron. The new brand was stamped to the side. Then they had to roll him over to vent the brand on the other side. The boy lay in a clumsy sprawl across the animal's neck as Lanahan finished the chore.

Without looking at him, Lanahan sent a hail at the riders. When they turned questioningly, he thrust both hands above his head, fingers clenched, thumbs straight up. The quitting signal.

'Let's call it a day,' he said to the boy. He tossed the iron toward the fire, waited until the lad loosed the ropes. The steer scrambled up, full of fight, and Lanahan had to duck behind Jed's hazing horse. The kid walked stumbling over toward the fire, sat down, and then lay back flat on the ground, a whistling expulsion of breath his only sound.

Tennessee came up at an easy lope, spotted the kid, and shook out a loop. He shot it out, not much bigger around than the brim of his hat, and caught the lad's feet. Bud Armishaw came to a sliding halt and swung down, whooping shrilly.

The boy kicked and scrambled, but Tennessee took a quick dally on his saddle horn and moved his horse a little to keep the kid stretched.

Bud yelled, 'Boss, here's one we missed. Git the iron, somebody!' He got an arm, flipped the lad over on his belly, and put his weight on him to hold him. Oscar Whitestaff ran to the fire, caught up the iron, brought it back. He spat on it, and the iron sizzled and sent up a little spurt of steam. The kid wasn't making a sound, but his bony body was heaving in a constricted bucking motion, and Bud was hard put to hold him.

'Ready,' Bud said. Oscar scuffed his boots noisily, and moved forward, and then Jed Martindale picked up a stick from the wood pile and pressed the blunt end of it firmly against the seat of the boy's pants. Oscar touched the iron into the water bucket.

It made an outrageous noise. The kid gave a great convulsive leap that unseated Bud, and he came around fighting, a white line showing around his mouth, but making no sound.

Then he saw the grins on their faces, the

stick in Jed's hand, the steaming iron at the bucket below his feet. He blinked rapidly, and the stiff line of his mouth broke. As his face began to pucker, Jed Martindale roughly cuffed the lad's hat down over his eyes and said gruffly, 'You're all right, Beans. If you got strength enough to carry me over to my horse, I b'lieve I can make it to the grub pile.'

As quickly as that, it was done. One of them threw the rope off his feet, and another helped him up. A couple of them dusted him off, with full-armed sweeps that nearly knocked him off his feet. But without putting it into words, with no gentleness or sympathy at all, they told him he was in. He was one of the bunch, and his name was Beans, and if he couldn't cut 'er, he could sure as hell chaw till she busted.

Jed Martindale cocked a quizzical eye at Lanahan, who gave him a short, tight grin and said, 'Still think I should have spelled him this afternoon?'

Jed said nothing, knowing it was true. It had been a tough test—and if the kid had cracked, they'd have pitied him. A man can't live with pity; not if it's going to be twenty-four hours a day for nearly a thousand gruelling miles. Beans was in.

CHAPTER SEVEN

The unseasonable hot weather broke. The clouds piled up and burst with their heavy cargo of water. No shower, this, but a steady sullen rain that lasted a week. The wind that had been a blessing during the hotter days was a chilling curse to the crew. Branding fires smoked sulkily, ate reluctantly at the underside of sodden sticks, and an iron had to be too hot when it left the fire in order to be not quite hot enough when the brand was burned. The thick grass turf was soon trampled down, and the ground men were mud-smeared head to foot, so chilled they welcomed a snuffy animal that made fight enough to warm them.

Lanahan rode up to the Prathers' wagon and swung down, his long greaser coat crackling. He shucked it off and threw it over the saddle to keep it dry, and mounted the steep steps.

'Come,' said Prather at his knock. The wagon was steamy inside with warmth. Eileen was stirring something on the little stove, her sleeves pushed up over her elbows. Prather lay on his bed, bright-eyed and flushed, but with his eyelids curiously sleepy over his shiny eyes.

He motioned toward a short bench against

the wall at the foot of his bed, but Lanahan gave Eileen a little smile and said, 'I don't dare interfere with the cook,' and remained standing.

Prather raised his eyebrows questioningly.

'We're not outfitted right,' said Lanahan bluntly. 'The chuck wagon is all right, though it needs a little work done on it for the long haul. We'll need another wagon, a good one, for a wood and bed wagon. That'll mean another driver, if I can get one, though the nighthawk can do it. The chuck wagon has got to be stocked. And there'll be cash needed for running expenses on the way. These things ought to be thrashed out now.'

'Of course,' said Prather. He said a trifle huskily, 'Eileen, give me the little box, please.'

She brought a small metal lock-box, and Prather opened it and withdrew a heavy canvas-and-leather money belt from it.

'You'll find one thousand dollars in this,' said Prather. 'You will have to stretch it until you deliver the herd in Wyoming.'

'The deal was two thousand, I believe,' said Lanahan.

'When delivery is completed in Wyoming. This thousand is for current expenses. We will have our final settlement at the end of the drive.'

Lanahan hefted the belt. He kept a close scrutiny on the man until he was certain of the thought forming in his mind. 'You're busted,' he said bluntly. 'That ten-thousand-dollar bank order business was a bluff. You're drawing to a busted flush with one thousand iron men to back you.'

'I wasn't bluffing, Mr. Lanahan.'

'You are now. I'd like to hear what the banker'd say today, if I tried to cash a ten-thousand-dollar order on your account.'

Prather stared up at him frostily, his sleepy eyes suddenly sharp and alert. Then surprisingly, he smiled.

'You are too shrewd for your own good sometimes, Mr. Lanahan. Not that it makes any difference. I should think though, that you might have felt easier on the drive with the thought that you had greater resources to back you.'

Lanahan said bluntly, 'I never made a cent lying to myself. I'd rather know where I stand. All right, this thousand is the bottom dollar. Buying a wagon and supplies is going to make a dent in it. I'm going to have to refill the chuck wagon every chance I get going across. Any of 'em decides to bunch it and quit that puts my'—he cut a look at Eileen and amended—'catches me with a split stick. You've cut it too fine, mister, too damned fine entirely.'

'I have every confidence in your judgment, Mr. Lanahan,' said Prather blandly. 'I'm sure you can do it.'

'Damn sight more than I got,' grunted Lanahan. Then: 'You think you've really got me, don't you? I've got to hang on till I come to the payoff, you figure. Except maybe all I've got to do is tuck this'—he held up the belt—'in my pants and drive out my horses and leave you to whistle.'

'You could,' agreed Prather. 'Of course, I'd have the sheriff on you before you moved ten miles...'

'Yes,' agreed Lanahan in his turn. 'But before he got there I can think of six different ways I could cache the money where nobody'd ever find it.'

Eileen Prather said with a sudden, almost shocking violence, 'Why are you deviling him, Mr. Lanahan? If you are a thief, you have your money in your hand. If you are not a thief, why are you talking like that? Do you want him to beg you? Do you want us to get down and crawl and beseech you, please, Mr. Lanahan, do what you agreed to do? Is it part of the agreement that you have to browbeat and humiliate a sick man? Do you enjoy that sort of thing, Mr. Lanahan?'

It set Lanahan aback, and it brought a flare of his own temper to the surface.

'No,' he said. 'I don't enjoy it. I don't enjoy being sold a bill of shoddy goods either. What I said was a warning, and your dad knew it. He was feelin' for me with the knife, too. But since maybe you don't understand unless it's thrown in your teeth, here it is: I'm takin' this herd through if I have to do it with one hand helpin' me an' the choreboy ridin' point. An' when I get there I'm goin' to get my money or I'll tie up the herd and shoot every head in its tracks and watch 'em rot before you make a penny profit. Is that plain enough?'

He held his look on her long enough to satisfy himself that she wasn't going to answer him, and then he turned, thrust the door aside with an impatient hand, and touched the steps only once, descending.

He mounted in a forceful squeaking of leather, and heard Prather say from behind him, gently, 'Mr. Lanahan.

He pulled his mount around and held it, his temper once more under control, and said, 'Yes?' in a neutral voice.

'Mr. Lanahan, I do think I owe you an apology. I have used you to a certain extent, but I assure you, from necessity, and not from choice.'

'That's all right. We know where we stand. I just hate to be taken for a fool.'

'If I have given that impression, I regret it exceedingly.' He came closer, buttoning up his long coat. 'I spoke of necessity, a moment ago. It is more than that; it is desperation. You were quite right in your evaluation of the situation. All my plans hinge on your good faith. With this venture, it is all or nothing with me.'

'Sure,' said Lanahan. 'But you've cut it pretty fine. If you've got any bail money tucked down in the toe of your boot, you'd better figure on having to use it.'

Prather shrugged wearily, gave him a wry smile. 'All I've got is the joker for a hole card. With any kind of luck, I'll come out. If not...' he spread his hands palm upward—'then I draw that busted flush you mentioned.'

'And then,' said Lanahan gently, shrugging the crackling greaser coat to settle it on his shoulders, 'we can all put on our tin bills and start scratching with the chickens.' He reined away. 'I'll see what I can do about picking up a cheap outfit.'

* * *

He worked his crew hard and late, and when he finally left them riding slack and tired to their supper, he made another circle and tallied roughly what unbranded stock remained. He ate his own supper without really tasting it, turning the hundred and one things that needed doing in his mind, and afterward he rode down to the Prather wagon.

Eileen came out of the door and onto the steps, a coat around her shoulders like a cape.

'Dad's asleep,' she said. 'Is it something important?'

'We'll finish up tomorrow,' he said. 'I expect I'll be going into Baker City some time after noon, if he wants something.'

'I'll tell him.' Her face and figure were indistinct in the near-dark, but he could see that she was looking at him most directly as she said, 'I'm sorry, Mr. Lanahan. I should apologize for the way I spoke to you.'

He had never heard her speak so softly, or so humbly, and it sent him into a wondering silence of nearly complete surprise. Then he found his tongue and said, 'That's all right. I've got a rough tongue myself; shouldn't have laid it on so hard.' He cursed himself for saying it so curtly, but could not recall the words now. He saw her lean slightly toward him, and then reach back to open the door and let light spill out over herself, catching him just in the outermost edge of the rectangle of light.

'I wanted to see your face,' she murmured surprisingly. 'I can't tell what you feel by your voice.'

'I mean well enough,' he said. 'I said what I meant.'

The mellow light was good to her; it touched on the bits of rain caught in her thick glossy hair and turned them to faintly glowing jewels; it showed her face half in shadow, still faintly, sweetly flushed by the warmth of the wagon she'd just left. It touched gently on the red curve of her lips, and he was suddenly uncomfortable facing that light, and he scrubbed at his whiskered jaw. *I'll have to shave*, he thought. *A man gets too slipshod when he's working*. He saw the faintest hint of a smile touch her shadowed lips, and wonder in a moment of small panic if he had spoken his thought aloud, but she said merely, 'Yes, I think you mean it, Mr. Lanahan.'

Something made him say, gruffly, 'Most people call me Clay.'

'All right,' she said, but did not use his name. 'Do you suppose I could ride in with you, when you go to Baker City?'

'Sure,' he said. 'We'll be taking the chuck wagon.'

He hesitated a moment, waiting for he knew not what, and then when she did not speak, he said, 'Well,' touched his hat and wheeled his horse away. 'I'll have Eben pick you up tomorrow.' He heard the door close behind him, but he did not look back. He shaved that night, looked up once to see Tennessee eyeing him and grinning faintly. Lanahan gave him a killing look, cut himself, and swore. Tennessee chuckled softly.

* * *

Oscar Whitestaff set the iron. Smoke puffed

up, and the outraged animal kicked and bawled. Oscar whooped suddenly and threw the iron in a careless pinwheel in the direction of the fire. 'That's the one we been lookin' for,' he shouted. He helped the hold-down man loose the ropes, and as the cow scrambled to her feet, Oscar drew back and aimed a prodigious kick at her rump, a kick that missed by a foot and spun Oscar half around on his high heels. 'The last one,' whooped Oscar. 'Bless her nasty scabby hide, the last one!'

Lanahan made an entry and slapped the little notebook closed. 'Two thousand and six,' he announced. 'You boys done real good. Let's go get a bait.' He grinned around at them.

'Now that we're done fooling around,' he said gibingly, 'we can go to work.' They made disgusted sounds, according to their various natures and caught horses for the ride to the chuck wagon.

The rain had stopped, but the leaden sky still pressed down close and threatening, and the wind had a stiff bite. Tennessee came over to Lanahan with a filled plate and cup and hunkered down alongside. There was nothing dry to sit on.

He said, 'I'd like to draw a few dollars and hit the big city this afternoon. Beans said he'd like to go too.'

Lanahan said, 'You're riding herd this

afternoon, aren't you?'

'Oscar and Bud said they'd take our shift. They're saving up for Boise.'

'All right,' said Lanahan. 'How much do you want to draw?'

'Twenty will do for me. Don't know about Beans.'

Lanahan nodded. He called across the fire, 'Ebe, you got any more chicken left?'

'Sure,' growled the cook. 'Millions of 'em.' He dug a huge iron spoon into a pot and lifted it heaping with beans. 'Come and git it.'

CHAPTER EIGHT

Eileen Prather rode the high seat of the chuck wagon beside Eben; and an extra team was led behind on picket ropes. Beans, Tennessee and Lanahan rode flanking the wagon. As they split up at the big general store, Tennessee said, 'Ebe, don't forget the strawberries.'

Eben retorted truculently, 'What kind you like best? The little white navy strawberries or the plain old brown ones?'

'Better get some of each. And a ham-hock. I do dearly love strawberries with a ham-hock in 'em.'

Eileen looked back and forth at their

deadpan faces and looked puzzledly at Lanahan. He grinned.

'Cowboy humor,' he said. 'We'll pick you up at the Western Hotel when we leave.'

Tennessee swung down quickly to help her over the wheel, and pulled off his hat. 'Can I escort you anywhere, Miss Prather?' His even white teeth flashed, but his yellowish hawk eyes were steadily upon her.

She gave him a little smile, and said, 'No, thank you. I don't think you'd be much interested in millinery.'

'Why,' he said, and his smiled flashed wider, 'I can't think of anythin' that'd interest me more.'

Lanahan saw her weighing the remark in her mind, but Tennessee's face was guileless, and she said a little stiffly, 'No, thank you,' and walked away from them. Tennessee watched her walk, appreciatively, and turned back, his thin lips puckered in a soundless whistle.

Lanahan said evenly, 'Sometimes you crowd your luck too far, Tennessee.' He dug into a pocket for a twenty-dollar gold coin he had previously removed from the money belt.

Tennessee's eyes came up and fastened closely on Lanahan's. 'An' what do you mean by that?' he asked in a flat murmur.

Lanahan flipped the double eagle to him. 'Just thought you'd better let Beans be your banker,' he drawled easily. 'He's not so likely to gamble it away on one spin.'

Tennessee kept that still, intent look on him a moment longer, and then again his reckless smile flashed, 'Luck's no good to you less you use it,' he said.

'Yeah,' said Lanahan dryly. He paid Beans, and saw the boy's eyes go a little round at the heft of the heavy gold coin. *Probably the most money he ever had in his hand in his life*, he thought. 'Don't spend it all in one place,' he said.

The kid gave him an uncertain smile, and then Tennessee took him by the arm. 'Come on, cow nurse,' he said. 'I'll point you in the right direction, and then you can catch your own rabbits.' They tramped off down the planked walk together.

Lanahan bought a used, but sound Studebaker wagon at H. Dale & Co., along with harness for a four-horse team. It made a dent in the money belt. He dealt out gold and bills from a pocket of the belt, got his receipt, and turned away from the counter buttoning his shirt. 'I'll be back for it in an hour or so,' he told the man. 'Just throw the harness into the wagon.'

He tramped down to the store where Eben was stocking the chuck wagon, and paid that bill. 'Get plenty of tobacco,' he told Eben. 'Half of them will be out of smoking in a week, and there's no stores out in the desert.'

He bought himself some shaving soap, tobacco, a couple of shirts, a box of cartridges. He tossed them inside the chuck wagon, and stood a moment, driven by an obscure restlessness but undecided as to destination.

It was time the herd was on its way. The Snake would be rising, fed by melting snow in the Bitterroots, and this herd would be a humdinger in case of trouble. He stopped in at Torrey's Saloon, had a drink without seeing a familiar face in the place and went on out, still restless.

Eben was loading the chuck wagon with the last of the supplies, but didn't know where Miss Prather had gone, nor Beans or Tennessee. 'I ain't nobody's nursemaid,' said Eben ungraciously.

'You are so right,' agreed Lanahan. 'You can haul out for the camp whenever you're loaded. I'll bring the other wagon. If you see any of the others, you can tell them I'm over at Dale's.'

'I'll tell 'em, but dollars to flapjacks you won't see 'em till you dig 'em out of some deadfall.'

Lanahan said in a shocked voice, 'You mean Miss Prather...'

Eben growled bearlike, 'Dammit, why don't you go away and quit devilin' a man when he's workin'?'

Lanahan went away.

For a moment he thought of looking up Tennessee and Beans, then decided to go and hitch up the new wagon and take it around to the Western Hotel. A man came out of the saloon behind him, and Lanahan had a sudden sense of familiarity, then remembered that he'd seen the man at H. Dale's, where he'd bought the wagon.

Lanahan angled across the spongy street that was still undecided whether it should be mud or dust, orienting himself. It was a long block's walk around the two corners. A narrow slot showed between two buildings, leading back to the alley, and he took the short-cut, ducking his head and buttoning his sheepskin coat as the chill wind whipped through the slot and stirred up the eye-smarting grit of the town.

Something warned him. Maybe it was the sound of a boot scuffling, not loud enough to hear except subconsciously, maybe just a sense of someone near. He half turned, and a voice, roughened a little with a taut excitement said, 'Hold it.'

He saw the gun in the man's hand then, raked frantically to get his own, under the hip-length sheepskin, and then the man hit him across the head with the barrel of the gun.

Lanahan ducked, tipping his head forward instinctively, and the wide brim of his hat took some of the curse off. But not all. The ejector button of the pistol made its own little streak of pain below the numbing shock of the blow, and he found himself in a sort of stupid surprise sitting back on his haunches with his hands braced out to the sides in the litter of the little slot.

It was all so dull and dreamlike. He felt a tugging at the front of his buttoned coat, and sluggishly raised a hand, but somehow had little control over it. He rolled over, feeling bundled-up and helpless, and then pain took a deep harsh bite on him. There was a coldness across his belly, and fire in his head, but he got an elbow under him and rolled, knowing dimly that his man was gone, hearing the scuff of his retreating run.

Then concussion beat at him, clubbed at his ears with a balled fist, and he came to hands and knees, shook his head like a dog coming out of water.

His clearing vision saw the man first, twenty feet away, shoulders braced against the side of the slot, legs braced awkwardly under him, and then the man was coming down, sliding his back flat down the side of the rough board wall, heels plowing a slow, deliberate furrow across the slot. As his rump hit the ground, he toppled stiffly toward Lanahan, showing the uneven parting of his hair.

While Lanahan was still trying to make sense of this, he saw Tennessee stepping catlike along the slot, his gun held waist-high, muzzle tipped a bit upward as if to let the little curl of smoke drift free of the muzzle. Tennessee stooped, came up with the thick snake-body of the money belt, and only then did his eyes come full on Lanahan, reckless and hot. A mirthless smile lifted the corners of his thin lips.

'Well, boss man,' he said in a tight little singing tone, 'you don't look so good.'

Lanahan felt wondrously stupid. His mind was slow, trying to make sense of it all, and he concentrated on getting his feet under him. He came up, swaying, feeling a little sickness inside, feeling also the coldness of the wind on his belly under his unbuttoned coat and shirt.

His head was clearing—enough to make a picture of it. The man—the nameless one yonder—had seen the money belt and made a slugging holdup of it. Tennessee had caught the tag end of it, and shot the man. But had there been one shot or two? Couldn't remember.

But there was Tennessee, his yellow hawk eyes alight with the tension that came with killing a man...

'Thanks,' said Lanahan. 'That was a tough one.'

Still the little mirthless smile lifted the thin corners of Tennessee's lips. 'Don't thank me—yet,' he said in his soft flat voice.

Lanahan lifted a hand, felt the taut sore ridge along the side of his head, the rip just below the hairline where the ejector button of the man's gun had struck.

Tennessee still stood, the thick belt hanging limply from one hand, hefting it a little with that stiff little smile. A nice stake in that belt. Better than two long years' wages for a rider's regular pay of thirty a month, gold and greenbacks. And Lanahan had a sudden feeling that this was not the first time Tennessee had held another man's money in his hands...

'Maybe,' said Lanahan slowly, 'I've made another mistake.'

* * *

The slow forward movement of time had stopped, it seemed to Lanahan. Maybe it was the steadily tightening band of pain around his head. Like a wintering river, the surface was the same as always, and perhaps it was underneath—but it was not water that glinted, but ice, holding every little ripple in arrested motion, stark, clean, immobile.

Then time broke, and blurred in motion again, and Tennessee was hefting the weight of the mney belt consideringly. Lanahan said in a voice that sounded vague and fuzzy to his own ears, 'Strictly speaking, it's not my money, Tennessee.'

'Strictly speakin',' said Tennessee, 'it's nobody's money, if you can't hang on to it. You see, money never has no mammy. It don't come running to suck, and it ain't got no brand. Money is a maverick, boss man. How much would you say was in here?'

Lanahan said, fighting off the fuzziness in his brain, 'What's left of a thousand. Why don't you count it?'

'Why, strictly speakin',' said Tennessee, 'it ain't my money either.' He grinned faintly, watching Lanahan with his confident yellowish eyes. 'It ain't passed enough hands to be a business deal, yet. You got it from Prather, an' this joker taken it off'n you, an' I taken it off'n him, but it's still got a kind of honest smell to it.'

His eyes were closely on Lanahan's as if making a decision. Then in a gesture that was shocking in its very casualness, Tennessee tossed the belt to Lanahan.

'I come higher than that,' he said with that mocking laughing lilt to his voice. He jerked his head back toward the body of the man behind him. 'The difference between me and him.'

'Yes,' said Lanahan slowly. 'Thanks.'

He stooped, feeling a giddy rush of blood to his head, and got his hat, wondering, *What made him change his mind?* He wadded the belt, jammed it into a side pocket of his coat, and buttoned his shirt. 'Come on,' he said to Tennessee, and moved out through the scattering of people who had come crowding around the end of the little alleyway at the noise.

A man wearing a badge came pushing through to meet them. He demanded sharply, 'What's up here? Just hold everything now, till we get squared away.'

Lanahan told him, as simply and straightforwardly as possible. The deputy looked at him closely.

'Sounds all right, but you'll have to come along and talk to the marshal. Both of you. Just walk ahead of me.'

He chose a man he knew out of the crowd to guard the body against disturbance, and walked carefully behind them to the marshal's office, where Lanahan and Tennessee retold it. Then they went back—marshal, deputy, the coroner who had been summoned from his business, Lanahan and Tennessee.

The coroner made a perfunctory examination, the marshal had the alley cleared and had them re-enact in part the details of the thing, and then the coroner said, 'Well, I guess we won't need much more of a hearing. I'll have to have your sworn statements, though.'

'My God,' said Lanahan out of the ringing depths of his fiercely aching head, 'it'd of been a hell of a lot less trouble to just let him have the money, wouldn't it? How many times you want us to say it?'

'This won't take long.' The coroner searched himself, came up with a pad of paper, scribbled rapidly for some moments, then read aloud what he had written. 'That about it?'

'Close enough,' said Lanahan.

'Raise your right hands,' said the coroner. He swore them to truthfulness. 'Sign here,' he said.

Lanahan signed.

'All right,' said the marshal, 'you can go. But I may be calling on you again, if anything turns up.'

'All right,' said Lanahan. He stood a minute, before he remembered his original intentions, and then said, 'I'll get the wagon. You see if you can find Miss Prather. I want to get back to the herd.'

'It'll be a pleasure, boss man,' said Tennessee.

'Sure,' said Lanahan dryly. Then he looked closely at the man and for the first time saw the strain and tension on him, the small signs of stress and careful self-restraint against showing it, and remembered that Tennessee had killed a man within the last few minutes and likely felt more than he showed. 'You want a drink?' he said suddenly. 'I think I could stand one.'

Tennessee smiled tautly. 'No,' he said, not

pretending to misunderstand. 'I can hold it this way. I get a couple drinks in me and loosen up an' God only knows which way she'll blow.' Then his thin smile stretched. 'Besides, I'll be callin' on a young lady. Want me smellin' like a saloon?'

'All right, do it your way. But, Tennessee—thanks.'

'Sho. Spect you'll do me one some time. Forget it.' He wheeled away then, quickly, almost eagerly, as if he couldn't wait to get away. Lanahan watched his whipslim back disappear, shook his head, and went to harness up. He caught Eben and the chuck wagon a short distance out of town, traded rigs, and sent Eben back for the others. He somehow didn't want company or questions just now. His head ached dully.

The marshal didn't come out to the herd, but the sheriff did. A quiet, steady-eyed man, hefty and soft-spoken, he hunkered down by the fire, asked substantially the same questions the others had, and finally nodded.

'I can see you didn't have much choice,' he said to Lanahan. To Tennessee, across the fire, he said, 'I can't hold anything against you, either. But I'll have to ask you to turn your gun in to the marshal next time you go in to Baker City, and leave it with him while you're in town. You understand.'

Maybe it was the flickering of the fire that gave Tennessee's eyes that dancing glint,

'No,' he murmured, 'I don't understand. That holdup artist had a gun. Take 'em away from the rest of 'em, and I'll turn mine in. Not before.'

The sheriff's quiet face was smooth and bland, showing nothing as he looked carefully across the fire. Lanahan said, 'No need to worry about it. We're moving the herd out at daylight. We've got no more business in Baker City.'

'All right,' said the sheriff. 'Good luck.' He took a cup of coffee from Eben then, and rode out a minute later.

Lanahan walked over to the Prather's wagon. Eileen answered his knock, and said, 'Come in.'

Prather had a high flush, and his skin looked dry and shiny. Even his voice was dry and whispering. He put his bright, but strangely sleepy eyes on Lanahan and asked, 'Everything all right?'

'Sheriff gave us a clean bill,' said Lanahan. 'We'll move out at daylight. Anything else I can do for you?'

Prather said vaguely, 'No, no. Just use your own best judgment. Good luck.' He put out a hand, and Lanahan took it. It felt like sun-dried rawhide that had been left near a fire. Lanahan said, 'Thanks,' nodded to Eileen, and stepped outside.

She followed him. 'I hope it goes well,' she said.

He shrugged, and gave her a little smile and a murmur of thanks, then asked seriously, ‘Have you had a doctor for him?’

‘He won’t let me send for one,’ she said. ‘But I’ll drive the wagon in to Baker City tomorrow, and he’ll have to go.’ He nodded approval, knew it was time to go, but still stood, looking down at her with a confused feeling that had a strange warmth in it, a sudden wish to appear in a better light to her.

‘Look,’ he said awkwardly, ‘if there’s anything I can do ... I know you don’t like me, but if I can help...’

She smiled at him suddenly, her head tipped back so that the faint starlight caught her eyes. ‘I’m sorry for some of the things I said to you,’ she said. ‘I have changed some of my ideas about you. You are not a very likable man, Mr. Lanahan. You are as hard to come near as a cactus, but I don’t think you are that way all the way through. I’ve seen you with the men, and especially that boy they call Beans. I am sorry if I have wronged you, really I am.’ She put out a hand impulsively, and he took it, feeling the warmth and firmness of it run all through him, and then suddenly he remembered Homer Flagg, and the warmth was gone.

‘Thanks,’ he said a little stiffly, ‘and good-by. I probably won’t be seeing you until we hit the Territory.’

'Good-by,' she said, and he wheeled away and tramped back to the fire, a peculiar confusion within him.

CHAPTER NINE

The weather got in one last good lick. The rain chilled, thickened, and then snow came, wet angry snow that was half melted by the time it hit the ground, but which came fast enough to make a soggy sheet on the earth. George Bristow rode up to Lanahan, shuddering a little even in a blanket coat under his slicker. 'Short summer, wasn't it?' he demanded bitterly. 'This is some weather for May.'

'They got a saying,' drawled Lanahan, 'that the man who tries to prophesy Oregon weather is either a fool or a newcomer. How long you been here, George?' George grunted savagely and reined back to his post.

The freak storm blew out as fast as it began. Two days' drive from the Snake, the sun broke through, scattering the clouds, and the wet earth steamed, holding the mist with its chill, so that the cows waded hock-deep in a carpet of curling white cotton. The two wagons trundled off to the side, drew ahead easily past the slow lag of the herd. Eben Longquist handled his chuck wagon, and the nighthawk, who spent his lonely nights in charge of the grazing horse herd, drove the wood and bed wagon. He came off his shift, sleepily wolfed his supper—breakfast for the rest—hitched up the wagon, and drove ahead to the next night's bed grounds, eight or ten miles, to crawl into his blankets and sleep until he was awakened in the late afternoon. He drew an extra ten dollars a month for his topsy-turvy extra work, and seemed satisfied with it.

There was work enough for the rest of them. It was a slow herd. In this flat land they could look back at noon and see where they had eaten breakfast though they pushed the cows a little, to discipline them to the drive.

The Snake was up—way up. Lanahan rode ahead, vaguely grateful for the warmth of the sun on his shoulders, and took a look at it. She was muddy, she was wide, and she was carrying loose drift down her wide gullet. Leaves and bark and ragged logs and brush that had washed in from caving banks upstream. And far out in the center a crest rode, like a spine, not crashing or roaring, but murmuring quietly with hidden strength. Lanahan dismounted, thrust a twig into the bank at water line, and hunkered morosely, watching it. Two cigarettes later, the twig was enough deeper to show a definite rise in the current. Lanahan sighed disgustedly and flipped his cigarette away.

Tennessee, riding point, inquired, 'How does it look?'

'We're a month late—or a month early. She's higher than a cat's back.' He gave Tennessee a little grin. 'Tie your hat down,' he advised. 'You'll be in deep enough for it to float before you're done.'

There was no midday meal that day. Eben had to make a ten-mile swing to the ferry to get the wagons across, and the crew had a smoke and a drink of water for lunch. They brought the lead cattle to the river shortly after noon.

Lanahan unbuckled his gun belt, untied his coat and slicker from behind his saddle, and tossed them to Beans. He yanked his hat down over his forehead, and moved his horse out into the water.

The horse stepped high and gingerly, the first few splashing steps, and lowered its head to snort at the water suspiciously. Lanahan eased him ahead. The first touch of water was like ice, pouring into the tops of his boots, and he whopped and drove the horse full into the current, preferring a quick plunge to this freezing by inches. He gasped as the water washed over him waist deep. The horse lunged out of the pothole, hit ground only once more, and then was in swimming water. Lanahan kicked out of the saddle and paddled, hanging to the saddle horn with one hand, the biting chill of the water tying his belly muscles in knots.

The shore slid by with astonishing speed, and a hatful of water caught him in the face and strangled him. Something struck his trailing legs, and he kicked out frantically to try to clear the tangle of submerged brush from the horse's driving legs.

Then the crest was past, and they did not drift so fast. He yanked the animal's head to a point more upstream, and they beat against it until suddenly the horse was scrambling on bottom. He plunged ahead, eager to get ashore, and as Lanahan's upper body came out of the water, the wind cut in through his soaking shirt with an icy knife.

He swung up, grunting as his streaming pants hit the sodden saddle, and the horse lunged through the shallows, snorting prodigiously. He let it keep moving against the chill, and sighted across the river, and shook his head in foreboding. He had lost more than the width of the stream in his drift, and he had been swimming a stout horse. And the crossing looked as good here as any place.

Then he shrugged. *No use crying, me boy*, he told himself, *your tears will make it just that much deeper*. He shivered at the thought, but he drove the reluctant horse back into the flood.

He emerged dripping and shuddering,

water slopping up in little squirts from the top of his boots at every rough trotting stride of the horse.

He pulled up, made his teeth stop chattering with heroic effort, and managed a grin. 'Damp,' he said wryly.

Tennessee looked at him and said broodingly, 'If I'd just had stake enough to make one more spin on that wheel...'

'G'wan,' retorted Lanahan gruffly, 'it's no worse than the Red coming up the Chisholm.'

'I crossed in a boat,' said Tennessee primly.

'You'll swim this one,' said Lanahan. 'Let's string 'em out.' He rolled his gun belt and sheepskin coat in a tight bundle, kneaded it into a taut sausage with his slicker, turned the ends back, and lashed it as tightly as he could.

He swung back into the saddle as they started the leaders of the herd down towards the bank in a long column.

'George,' called Lanahan, 'you look like you'd float pretty high in the water. You and Tennessee and I work the water. Point 'em high, towards that patch of brush yonder. Beans, you and Jed work this bank. Keep 'em coming, but no more than six or eight wide; I don't want any bunches big enough to start a mill. Let's go!'

Jed, across the point of the herd, couldn't

hear, but he knew his job. At Lanahan's jerky wave, he crowded in, whooping and snapping the tag end of his catch rope, and hazed the leaders into the water. They bawled and floundered, but with Jed on one side, and Tennessee and George on the other, they went; and suddenly they were in swimming water, noses cocked high, an occasional rolling heave showing shoulders sleek and wet as otters. Lanahan took the plunge again, pointing his mount's head a bit more upstream this time.

Again the crest took its rolling lunge at them, but the horse, a big Oregon roan, swam like a swamp rabbit. He came lunging up onto solid footing as if he could do that job all day. But Lanahan held him to the water, belly deep, giving the swimming cattle an aiming point, while he loosed his catch rope with stiff fingers and shook out a loop.

The cattle were coming. He could see Tennessee, head and shoulders above the saddle, on the downstream side of the leaders, saw the water spurt up as Tennessee lashed with a short bight of his lariat to keep them headed up. A wonderful thing, the herd instinct. Keep the leaders headed, and the rest would do all they could to follow. But they were swinging down fast, too fast, as the ridge of current put its watery shoulder to them and began its slow powerful heave.

Tennessee was yelling. Even above the hissing grumble of water Lanahan could hear his high tenor voice. His lashing arm rose and fell, and water spurted up under his rope. Lanahan cocked the loop of his own wet rope, and crowded his mount back out into the water, shoulder deep. The leaders passed the crest, and in the easier water, Tennessee was bringing them a little more upstream, so that the string across the water turned up a bit, like an uncompleted giant 'U.' The leaders were still a little downstream, and Lanahan moved that way, waited until he could get a fair throw, saw the head steer's bulging, rolling eyes behind snorting, upflung nostrils, and made his cast. The loop settled over the animal's horns, and instantly Lanahan swung his horse toward the bank, quartering upstream, towing the lead steer behind him. The scrambling horse splashed through knee-deep water, then fetlock-deep, and then was out onto the easy slope of the bank. The rope, soaking wet, would not shake free, and Lanahan had to dump the steer and lean down to twitch the loop loose while the downed animal was still trying to figure out what hit him.

Tennessee had gained the bank by the time Lanahan got back, and was giving his horse a breather. He looked like a sopped rag, with every fold of his clothing streaming water, and he shook his head in silent resignation as Lanahan plunged back in to bolster the sagging curve of swimming cattle.

It took quite a while. Two thousand head, strung thin, made a tremendous line, and they were all soaked before it was done. Lanahan changed horses twice that afternoon, and lost count of how many times he crossed the river. He sent the boy Beans across, making him take the upstream side over the lad's protests, and gave him the comparatively easy job of loose-herding the tired cattle that had crossed.

The weak ones were bad. They played out, and with the placid indifference of tired cattle, simply gave up to the remorseless strength of the river and were carried away downstream. Then it was swim and rope and drag, with the horses gamely fighting the double load; and, with typical perversity, the cow which so calmly let the river take her, fought like a tiger when a man tried to loose the rope that had saved her life.

But eight men couldn't be in enough places at once. Inevitably one got away, hurried along on the current beyond rope-cast. She'd have made it alone maybe, but a swirl of current took her into and under an arm of loose drift that hung out from a point downstream, and she was gone. Three in a bunch, a little later, who made slack water under a steep-cut bank, swam and pawed at the shelving bank, then gave up and drifted before a man could be released from the pressure of work to try to save them. The horse herd crossed without mishap.

Tally two thousand and two—wet and weary, eyes bulging like Bermuda onions with the scare and effort, but ashore in good shape. *String 'em out! Move 'em along. Be the good Lord willin', if there's water, if there's grass, we'll take 'em through. Hi-yi You slab-backed, bellerin', wall-eyed skites; git along, git along—for Wyomin' will be your new home . . .*

Feed good, water good; following the general course of the Snake where it made its long sagging loop across the Idaho Territory; eight miles a day, ten miles some days, June sun a little more than warm, but not too hot. Dust, working up under the scuffling hoofs, acrid dust smelling of cattle; the long sweep of the scrubby land; the winy spice of sagebrush in the nostrils; meadowlarks flipping themselves carelessly into the air to pour out their burbling liquid song; great mule-eared jackrabbits jinking in incredible sailing leaps, ten feet and better to the jump; the slow, grumbling, muttering, crawling progress of eight thousand cloven hooves—*Git along, there!*

Across the Weiser River. One cow lost, a knothead out of the drag, who didn't seem to care. The tangle of drift below the ford got her. Block up the wagons; no ferry. Flour and beans and sugar up under the canvas top on makeshift scaffolds. All the beds got wet in the other wagon, though. Sun so hot it didn't matter much. Grass starting to turn brown.

'Git along, there!'

CHAPTER TEN

Boise. A trading and transportation stop, with Fort Boise as its nucleus. Lanahan rode in beside Eben and the chuck wagon, bought a few supplies, collected a little mail. Lanahan did not get any letters, didn't really expect to—but he thumbed through the thin stack twice—just to be sure.

'Flagg herd?' The storekeeper rubbed a reflective hand across his chin. 'Oh, a month ago, maybe. Moving right along. Homer Flagg wasn't it? Reason I remember, he got a whole slew o' mail, all in the same handwritin'. How about some tomatoes? Got a good price on 'em, and a can o' tomatoes goes good out on the lava and alkali . . .'

Crossing the camas prairies they came on a man driving a peddler wagon, its contents a jumble of tinware and cloth bolts and odds and ends of hardware and trinkets. He drifted up and down the country, dealing with the few isolated grangers and shoestring ranchers and their wives, peddling his goods and swapping from the string of worthless-to-fair horses that came behind his wagon on an enormously long lead line, like fish on a stringer. He had trousers and army shirts and rank tobacco, and some of the crew replenished on things missing and Lanahan refused a dozen offers of horse trades.

Before the man moved on, he said, 'I'd watch them horses, mister. There was a drive ahead of your'n that had a little Injun trouble, an' they're some of 'em out an' projeckin' around to see what they kin turn up.'

'Bannacks?' said Lanahan in a tone of mild disbelief.

'Well, yup, an' some Paiutes. Them Paiutes is horse Injuns, an' they been tradin' down south for buttons, an' they been makin' mescal, an' some of the runchy young Bannack bucks been goin' along with 'em. They're feelin' pretty uppity, anyway.'

'Count of what?'

'Well, that other drive—big feller roddin' it—Flag brand—y' know them Bannacks, they still think this is their country, an' they kind of figger they got a beef comin', whenever they're hungry; so they hit this outfit up for some slow buffalo, an' he wouldn't give 'em none, an' when the Bannack head man got a little uppity, this big ramrod, he put the head man out of the camp at the end of the cook's blacksnake whip, an' I guess he warmed his hide pretty good. So them Bannacks, along with some Paiutes, I don't doubt, tried to cut a couple horses out of the cavvy that night, an' there was some shootin'. I don't think they killed any, but they crippled a couple of them Injuns, an' so between that an' the mescal an' the Paiutes, I'd be 'nclined to watch my cavvy, was I you.'

'Thanks,' said Lanahan. 'I'll do that.'

'No thanks necessary. Now look; I'll swap you that black mare an' that spotted geldin' fer that one roan. Now there's a deal fer you—two fer one.'

'Not today,' said Lanahan, 'but thanks, anyway.'

The peddler shrugged and drove on, and Lanahan passed the word on to the hands about the Bannacks.

Now, he thought, *there's our boy Flagg. He leaves a dirty nest behind*. He knew Flagg's brand—a rectangle at right angles to an upright line which made the flag staff; a smaller square inside the rectangle, upper left corner for the union—Flag brand; Flagg's Flag. *Very neat. Cute. Nice fellow. Should have shot the sonofabitch the first time he opened his mouth—saved a lot of trouble all around. Now I suppose nobody gets any sleep till we get off the Bannacks' range. Because Homer Flagg's too damned chinchy to give the Injuns a sore-footed drag he'd likely lose anyway, on the next water crossing.*

Hi-yi, you bellyachin' wonder—git along! Git along, there, or maybe I'll give you to the goddamn Bannacks, you slew-footed, sag-bellied . . . *Git along!*

After two undisturbed nights, with thirty miles behind them, Lanahan began to figure that the Bannacks had run out of mescal or perhaps the Paiutes had picked up and gone on, in their restless way. A wild yell and a booming shot out of the dark before dawn of the third day disabused that thought and brought the sleepers awake as explosively as flushed quail breaking cover.

Lanahan, sleeping fully dressed save for boots and hat, came out of his soogans still not half awake, and acting strictly from previous thought, snatched the .44 out of the holster hung across the horn of the saddle he used for a pillow, clawed a handful of cartridges out of the saddlebag, ran sock-footed as he roared an alarm to awaken anyone not already awake, and swung bareback onto one of the horses kept picketed just past the chuck wagon. The horse promptly bucked him off, but he held onto the coiled picket rope, got a fresh grip close to the halter as he followed its prancing circle and swung aboard again, lined it out and drove the animal out toward the cavvy. He could hear disturbance at the cattle herd, beyond the chuck wagon, but there was no sound of shooting, and there were two men on night-herd there. The threat seemed to be to the cavvy, at the moment.

A gaspipe-barreled musket spewed out a skyrocket flare of burning coarse black powder, and he pulled down on that and let go with the .44. His horse neatly side-stepped about a yard and nearly dumped him again, and he swore bitterly and promised himself there would be saddled animals held close for this sort of thing next time.

He sent a warning yell at the nighthawk and got the sharp-toned windy reply, 'Around on the north side! Goddam Injuns. Whole bunch of 'em!'

Lanahan yelled acknowledgment, bore hard left and bellied down on his reaching horse, trying to skylight something, anything, against a sky that was hardly a shade lighter than the earth. There wasn't much to see out there but plenty of blackness. His vision was still fouled by the flare of his last shot. He ran his horse another hundred yards, then hauled in to bring the horse to a restless, hoof-shifting halt. The cavvy seemed to be running in a hundred different directions, and out of that confusion and the yelling of someone else approaching from the camp, there was a steady *wham! wham! wham!* as the nighthawk fired his revolver at something off across the scattered cavvy.

Close by, Lanahan heard the grunting nervous sounds of a horse, heard plunging, to-and-fro movement above that snorting and rode at the noise. His vision was clearing from the gunshot-blindness. He caught a confused blur of movement ahead, yelled at it and got no reply, rode closer until he thought he saw a man shape as separated from the horse, and fired at it.

In the flare of the shot he caught a dreamlike glimpse, quickly blanked out, of a staring Indian face, an impression of nakedness and of fright; and then the horse shape broke away and ran, snorting thunderously, and only a soft padding came from the Indian's hard-running moccasined feet. Lanahan threw another shot out after that sound, drew no return fire, turned and rode back toward his own approaching men, yelling ahead to warn them of his coming before some taut-stretched one threw a bullet at him.

He caught the dim shapes of a bunch of four or five horses, rammed the .44 into his waistband, worked out the end of his picket rope for a persuader, and herded the animals ahead of him toward the campfire, which was flaring high after someone had thrown wood on it. He yelled ahead, 'I'm bringing in horses—catch 'em up!' and saw men come out, backlighted by the fire, noosed lariats ready.

When the horses were caught, he rode on into the camp, stamped into his boots, swung his heavy saddle on his own horse, bridled it, and found his gun belt.

'All right,' he said, 'Pair up. Beans, you go with Tennessee. Take the east side; head back anything you find. George, where's Tex? Oh. Well, get on back with those cows, and yell so he'll know you're coming. Eben, get out of that damn firelight! Get a rifle and keg up under the wagon. I'll be riding almost straight north, so don't anybody get nervous and shoot me. Anybody seen or heard from the nighthawk?'

Nobody had, since they'd seen him shooting last, and Lanahan rode out quickly, hailing the darkness, riding with his revolver poised muzzle upward in his right hand, fully reloaded and ready.

He found the nighthawk and rode on in his company, found a few small bunches of the scattered cavvy, headed them, turned them back and sent them toward the camp, hoping they'd keep to that course. Finally Lanahan called in his outriders and they returned to the camp, pushing what stock they could find ahead of them. There wasn't anything else they could do before daylight. Heartily, Lanahan damned the darkness, the cavvy, the Indians, Homer Flagg, and the whole louse-bitten mess. Then he went back and damned Homer Flagg again, for good measure.

A daylight tally showed four horses missing, one carrying a broken arrow with a saw-steel head in its ham, another limping from an attempted hamstringing, and others nicked, bruised and scarred from head-long chousing around in the dark. The cattle were scattered widely, a couple were down with arrows in them, but that was from pettish revenge. The Indians hadn't been after the cattle; they'd wanted those horses, but apparently they weren't even good sneak thieves, and they hadn't had the force or generalship that tougher plains Indian would have used.

Had they been Crow or Sioux or Cheyenne, likely they'd have come mounted, stampeded the cattle right over the chuck wagon and the sleeping camp, and made off with the cavvy like disciplined cavalry foragers. Still, the Bannacks now either had, or had driven off, four good cattle horses.

'Tennessee,' said Lanahan, 'you want to take a ride with me?'

'Let me get another cup of coffee an' some ca'tridges, boss man, an' I'm with you.'

They flushed their quarry before noon,

still traveling northward, roughly paralleling a nameless little creek, two riders driving a pair of horses before them.

Lanahan levered a cartridge into his rifle and said, 'This nag's got a little run left in it. I think I can head 'em. You hold right on 'em, and if they try to swing out by crossing the creek, shoot ahead of 'em and see if we can't keep 'em on this side.'

Tennessee said meagerly, 'All right, boss man,' and Lanahan put the big Oregon roan into a headlong gallop. The Indians, after a moment of milling indecision, started to make a run for it. He raised the rifle and lobbed a bullet in ahead of them. One of the Indians swung a short cap-and-ball musket toward him and touched it off in a billowing puff of white smoke and a distant boom.

The stolen mount, not used to bareback riding, already nervous with the strange wild Indian smell, dismayed by the gunfire, promptly humped its back and bucked. The Indian stayed with him for one jump and then went in a graceless sprawl over the animal's down-pitched neck. The horse lashed out with its heels and crow-hopped away, and the buck got up, started to run, fell down, got up again, and hobbled with a bad knee toward the nearest clump of creekbank willows. Tennessee yelled and fired with his revolver, coming in at a keen run. The Indian buck flinched, apparently at a near miss, hobbled in a short semicircle, yelled something at his retreating companion.

The one, apparently unarmed, seemed intent only on flight. At the hobbling one's call, however, he raised himself to look back, and Lanahan fired the rifle again, leading far ahead to keep from hitting the horse, and heard the bullet strike and ricochet. Then the fleeing Indian turned the horse clumsily, the horse nervously fighting to the Indian's reining which consisted of hauling its head bodily around by a hackamore rope.

Tennessee rode straight at the crippled buck, who at the last moment threw the empty musket at him and leaped aside to evade trampling; the mounted one came charging, shrieking a singsong chant, at the last moment snatching a twelve-inch butcher knife from his hip, driving in to close with Tennessee, who had rolled half out of his saddle to avoid the thrown musket. Tennessee lifted his arm and fired all in one motion, and the Indian screeched and fell headlong backward over the rump of his horse. Lanahan, charging in on a slight downslope, threw another rifle bullet at the cripple trying for the willows and missed. The buck stopped at the shot, turned, and stood, arms widespread in that position of crucifixion as Lanahan rode the last few hundred feet.

He kept the rifle on this one. Tennessee had pivoted his horse, brought it to a quick turning halt, and sat in his saddle now, staring down at the one he'd shot, his pistol trained on the figure.

Lanahan herded his cripple ahead of him, saw then that the other one was not dead either. Tennessee's snapshot had hit the knife arm, plowed completely through and lodged the bullet in the thick muscles above the collar bone.

The Indian's eyes were open, but swimmy with shock; and he watched Tennessee as he lifted the pistol, took aim, and then with a sudden breathless sound, lifted the revolver, let the hammer down to half-cock with a practiced snap of his wrist.

Lanahan said roughly, 'He'll never appreciate it. Figure you for a fool and an old woman for not killing him when you had the chance.'

'Sho,' said Tennessee in a strained voice, 'but my God, not in cold blood...'

'Hell, keep 'im for a pet, if you want,' said Lanahan. He rode at the one with the sprung knee, covering him with the rifle, indicated by gesture that he should throw away his belt knife, then dismounted and got both knives and the rusty trade musket. He found a rock, large enough and solidly bedded, and carefully and thoroughly beat the musket into splinters of wood and sprung, useless metal, then remounted.

'Well, make up your mind,' he said. 'Keep him or turn him loose. We got to get these horses back to the outfit.'

Tennessee gave him a thin humorless grin. 'Druther keep a pet polecat,' he said, and turned his mount to join Lanahan in gathering the loose horses. As they completed this and rode back, they could see the one standing, staring after them, while the wounded one was making feeble attempts to get up.

Tennessee said meditatively after long moments, 'Why is that now, you spose? I sure aimed to kill 'im with that first shot; wouldn't have bothered me a mite if I had of.'

'Why,' said Lanahan, 'you're just an old woman.'

Tennessee's narrow grin flicked on. 'Sho,' he said, 'I spose you ain't.'

Said Lanahan, 'I just figured to let mine grow a little bigger, till his hide is worth somethin'.'

Tennessee snorted. They drove the loose horses ahead of them at a comfortable walking gait. Neither of them spoke of it more than they had to when they rejoined the herd.

* * *

The herd trailed well enough. The two cows the Indians had shot were not a total loss for Eben butchered enough beef off them to last several days. They slept light for a week, but there were no more alarms in the night. Little by little the incident was almost forgotten in the monotony of the daily work.

The rough part's ahead, boys. Git along, there!

CHAPTER ELEVEN

Man, she was a mighty country. Mighty worthless, some would add. But big. Sawtooths poking up yonder, and the hazy hulk of the Smoky Range. Bitter sage and stark greasewood, and clumps of sun-cured grass none too plentiful, so that the herd spread wide and moved slow, and ate without relish of it. Dust winding and coiling and climbing to make its own enclosed world until a man rose aside and looked into the eye-stretching distances and then saw in perspective; this great miles-long, mile-high cloud was but a tiny wind devil's puny stirring; the great sprawling blot of the herd only a pinpoint on a many-specked map; the broad marked trail, scuffed and stirred and splattered with the elimination of these thousands of creatures, was but a smudged pencil mark on that same great map of an infinity of space.

A long day's drive and another camp, and it could have been last night's camp, or the night before that, for still the Smokies lay yonder, the Snake somewhere down there, the mighty land before and behind.

The man who named the Snake spoke truth. Tortuously looped, treacherous, friendless and unfriendly, rushing precious water through the high desert, but jealously guarding that water behind forbidding rough rock walls; furnishing no drink for man or beast or thirsty earth. Dry camps in the dust, almost within sound and sight of that water, when feeder creeks were sometimes too far apart for a day's drive with this slow herd; dry camps when the cattle moaned on the bed grounds, and stirred restlessly, and the circling night herders rode slowly and sang tunelessly to let the spooky cattle know just where they were every minute. The late shift went on early, and the first shift stayed late, to double the herders while the cattle went through their nightly ritual of the midnight stretch.

Normally, like a signaled maneuver, the herd got up, stretched, kinked their tails, sent little rippling shudders down their spines, while they gently grumbled; took a step or two possibly, and a mouthful of grass and lay down again.

Now, on dry camp, they moved restlessly, sometimes turning the stretch into a restless milling that lasted an hour or more. Spooky, edgy, half angered—unpredictable. Sore-footed, thin, drained down by the hard life without and the demanding life within. Then they started dropping their calves.

Beans, back in the drag, whistled shrilly, and made a beckoning wave of his arm. Lanahan rode up to look at the cow, her head lowered suspiciously, curved horns vaguely threatening the horses, while the spindly newborn calf butted enthusiastically at its breakfast.

'What'll I do?' Beans inquired helplessly. 'She won't herd, and the calf can't keep up, and all she wants to do is sneak out and keg up in the brush.'

Lanahan said resignedly, 'I knew it would be like this.' He shook out the loop in his rope and said, 'Drop a loop on her horns.' Together, they dumped her, and Lanahan pulled three feet together and tied them. He caught the calf after two tries, picked it up and boosted it up to Beans.

'Put it in the bed wagon,' he said. 'Then bring George or Tennessee when you come back. And stop by the chuck wagon and get that coil of soft-lay cotton rope.'

'The bed wagon?' inquired Beans.

'Yes,' said Lanahan. 'We'll have to build some kind of a pen in the back. Maybe we can save a few of them. Shag along, and don't forget the rope.'

That was the first one. After that, it was a daily chore. Rope the new mother, neck her to another cow, with a length of soft cotton rope, so that perforce she went with the herd. If the calf was a strong one, load it into the makeshift little pen in the back end of the bed wagon. Stake the calves out at night, so the cow could come and nurse it. A rough life; perhaps one in ten survive it. Some, of course, couldn't even make the attempt; the calf had to be destroyed, the cow necked to another and kept moving ... on into the lava desert.

* * *

Black land. Rock and powdery earth that was practically pure volcanic ash. July sun like a vast ball of burnished brass shimmering with its own super-heat. Air so dry and thin that the heat was magnified; air just full-bodied enough to hold the feathery black dust suspended, to let it slowly settle on a man's hide, to work into the damp folds of his skin, where it suddenly developed grating edges.

Two long days' drive—no water. Then shallow little pond, bitter with condensation; another day when a little sump and its tiny trickle of creek forced them to literally cut the herd into groups and water them fifty head at a time, a job that took a day, and strung the herd for two miles. Not a single calf born in those four days survived.

They attempted no other herding than keeping the cows in a reasonably sized group. Thirsty cattle will not graze; and when they tried to drive them, the cattle sullenly crowded into groups and milled aimlessly, or moved a few steps to halt again. In the cooler night, they would not bed down, finally started to move out.

The crew rubbed eyes with kerchiefs wet with water from the chuck wagon kegs, water as hot as if it had just come off a stove, and hit their saddles again. The herd moved four or five miles before it settled down about three o'clock in the morning.

Lanahan rode out ahead, early, blinking resentful red eyes at the hateful shimmering sun that peeked over the horizon. Even the horse made none of its usual exuberant bucking as the heavy double-cinch Texas saddle was tighened up. These horses, broken to the center-fire, single-cinch, Oregon rigs, protested the flank cinch rigs vigorously enough to wake their riders to full awareness every morning. Now the fresh animal, not ridden in four days, almost plodded, without fire or gumption.

The dust rode with them, for the wind was coming up from behind, and Lanahan wearily pulled his bandanna up around his face and accepted it dully. He held to the outer edges of the lava beds proper, scanning the earth in great sweeps for any sight of green that might mark water. Off to the side, the tortured lava was shaped in weird twists and turrets; and the breeze, playing far back in some hidden cavern of broken lava, vented a deep booming whistle, roared like a hurricane; then fell silent as suddenly as it began.

A desolate land—he saw no living thing save stunted scrub brush that was so dark green as to be almost black. Just dust, and scattered bunches of tenacious brown burned grass, the scrub, the sweeping, jumbled miles of jagged lava. Grit caked his teeth, and he worked his lips vainly to get up enough saliva to spit, finally scrubbed at them with the edge of his kerchief.

He rode into the camp in the dusky light of evening, heard the low, steady complaint of the herd, and compressed his lips. He swung down at the fire, not much bigger than a hat, where Eben held forth, and got a cup of coffee. The coffee wasn't much hotter than the water in the kegs, which had little satisfaction in it, but the coffee drove some of the tiredness out.

'I suppose it's no better up ahead,' said Eben truculently.

'Worse,' said Lanahan, and took another sip from the tin cup. Then Tennessee came around from behind the wagon to look at Lanahan queerly.

'We got company,' he murmured.

'What?' asked Lanahan, not really caring.

Tennessee jerked his head aside, a short beckoning motion, and Lanahan walked toward him. Tennessee pointed with his chin, without taking his hands from where they hung with thumbs hooked in his belt.

Beyond the chuck wagon, fifty yards out, was the unmistakable outline of the Prather wagon.

Lanahan raised a slow hand and rubbed it across his gritty jaw.

'She asked for you,' said Tennessee. His voice held a taut, questioning note that somehow irritated Lanahan's ears.

'Yeah?' he grunted, making the syllable blunt and challenging without looking at Tennessee. He got a short thick moment of silence and then a flat murmur, 'I was just passin' the word.'

'Sure,' said Lanahan in a neutral tone which neither retracted nor apologized.

He scuffed across the scabby earth, cuffed absently at his sleeves a couple of times, realized that nothing but a long bath and a shave and then another bath would make him presentable, and that it was too late to worry about it. He walked around the back corner of the wagon.

Eileen sat on the bottom step at the rear of

the wagon, not really looking at anything, simply sending a level gaze out into the dusk. Her hands were loosely clasped around her knees, and she looked up at Lanahan as the sound of his steps came to her. It was a blank look, as if she were coming back from an intense concentration, and her expression slowly changed from an intent gravity to a mechanical half smile that was as meaningless as the painted expression on a doll's face.

Lanahan said, 'This is unexpected, Miss Prather. How . . .' And then he knew, before he got the question out. Eileen tipped her head back a bit, still with that unchanging smile that was not a smile, and she said with a soft and quiet flatness, 'My father is dead, Mr. Lanahan. He died in Boise City.'

'Ah,' said Lanahan in a quiet shocked voice, 'that is too bad.' Instantly he felt himself a complete fool for having said it with such blatant triteness, and dredged his brain for something, anything, that would put his feelings into sensible words, and could not find them.

He stood uncomfortably before her close and evaluating look, feeling as if her eyes were flaying skin, drilling bone, probing deep into his brain itself for something.

'I'm sorry,' he said, feeling the words to be no less trite and meaningless, 'truly I am.'

Still she kept that closely searching, almost

impersonal probing look on him. 'Yes,' she said finally, rising from the step to stand before him.

'There is something for you inside,' she said. Her voice was flat, almost completely uninflected. 'Come in.'

She mounted the steps, and he followed, with the odd feeling of not quite wanting to. She searched high, to light the lamp, and the match went out before the wick caught. Lanahan dug up a match and struck it, and she stood, still reaching up to steady the lamp as he fired the wick. Her hand touched his, and it felt cold, deadly cold, and suddenly he found his fingers shaking. He whipped the match out brusquely, snapping his wrist up and down, finally snapping the match stick by crushing his thumb against the cooling head until the wood gave.

In the pale lamplight he could see that Amos Prather's bed had been stripped, and the bare bunk frame tipped up and chained to the side of the wagon. The whole interior had a feeling of bareness, dustiness, desertion, an unused air, though Eileen had almost certainly been living in it since Boise City. Still, there was a feeling of emptiness and silence, which made him say, 'How did you get here? You didn't drive all this way alone?'

'I came with a freighter's outfit part way. He was kind enough to give me a driver.

Then they turned off this side of the river, taking the southern route, through Fort Hall. I came the rest of the way alone.'

She said no more in elaboration, nor did she ask why his inquiry. He shook his head silently, turned a little away, and remembered his hat, which he dragged off and held in his hand.

Eileen reached across her bed and from a shelf above it took a thick folder tied with a red tape. From this she took an envelope and handed it to Lanahan. He accepted it, turned it over in his fingers, looked around, and dropped his hat on one of the upturned boxes which served for chairs.

He ripped open the envelope. The letter inside was undated, and it went:

Mr. Lanahan:

When you receive this, I shall be dead or incapable of acting for myself, and thus must take this means to communicate with you.

I have used you, in a manner in which I have never used any man, and I make no apologies. As I said to you once before, it was not from choice but from desperation. I must therefore continue to use you. I have an implacable beast eating at my vitals, and there is much to be done before it devours me entirely.

My daughter, by virtue of certain legal instruments already executed, is my sole heir and assign, and the executor of any estate remaining in my name. She is sole owner and proprietor of the herd, ranch and other appurtenances of the AP brand. This wording sounds braver than it really is, since all debts and liens will have to be assumed by her. It is pitifully little that I pass on from a lifetime of industry.

I cannot charge you strictly with an obligation which is only moral at best, when I am the one responsible for saddling you with this obligation without the slightest regard for your own interests. I cannot even beg of you as a dying man, as I have never humbled myself to beg of any man, without apprising you as honestly as I can, of the situation and how I have used you.

Some of it you have deduced. My Portland business was liquidated to purchase the scant buildings and holdings of the ranch in Wyoming Territory. The ranch was mortgaged to secure the money to buy the first Grande Ronde herd. This herd in turn was mortgaged to pay in part for those cattle delivered in Baker City. These monies, of course, were insufficient for my pyramiding transactions, and were augmented by the pledging of my word, worth little as it is, and secured by personal notes and due bills. Perhaps an ill man does not think clearly, but it was not until I was irretrievably committed that I learned how poor my own odds were in this fantastic gamble. In my innocence and ignorance, I assumed that bred cows would automatically increase my herds. I did not learn until too late the delicate and improvident nature of such a herd, for instance.

But this must not be an attempt to quibble and justify. Since my sorry legacy to my daughter is little more than indebtedness, I must beg of you to do all in your power to salvage what you can. Believe me, nothing I have done has been done to enrich myself. It was a dying man's attempt to secure some trifle of means and independence for those he leaves behind.

By means of one last bit of connivery, you will find on deposit in your name five hundred dollars, with Wells Fargo in Virginia City. I do not intend to discuss the ways and means of this last petty dishonesty, and I must pledge you never to mention it to anyone. Do not balk at it, for you will need it to continue and complete the drive. If the taint of it offends you, you may do what you wish with what remains when your obligation is completed.

I cannot demand anything of you. I can only humbly beseech.

In your hands is the power to destroy a lifetime's labor. In your hands is the power to destroy my reputation and all I have been able to give to my daughter. I pray, do not misuse it. I can say no more.

Yours most sincerely,
Amos Prather

* * *

Lanahan's own handwriting was of the rounded and schoolboyish method he had learned years back. He had some trouble deciphering Prather's angular script, particularly where the man's urgency had driven him to write more hastily than his weakened hand could perform. But by the time he had finished the four closely filled pages, he was swallowing dryly, and the pages were trembling in the hand he held up to gain all he could of the hanging lamp's light.

He lowered the letter finally, to find Eileen's eyes on him with a terrible intentness—a waiting, watchful, almost frightened look—and almost shamed, he looked away, down at the pages in his hand.

'Do you know what is in here?' he asked.

'No,' she said in a strained, almost whispering voice. 'He wrote it, and sealed it, and gave it to me. He said—he said—I was to give it to you. That was the day before he—died. I—I suppose it was his final instructions to you. Isn't that it?'

He looked down at the pages. 'No,' he said slowly. 'Not instructions. Not orders. He—begged me. Why me? Why should he...'

Quite suddenly, Eileen was crying. Her strictly disciplined face crumpled as her lips spread in a wide grimace of purest pain, and she cried, as a heartbroken child cries, not even bothering to turn her face away; cried almost silently, as if completely forgetful of her audience, of anything save the terrible hurt which was hers.

Lanahan watched helplessly, turned away, not wanting to witness this nakedness of grief; then turned back because there was nothing else to do save leave the wagon, wondering helplessly what he might do.

She stared at him with wide, blind, tear-filled eyes, and impulsively he put out one dirty hand, not really daring to touch her, but impelled by he knew not what into that gesture, and she swayed toward him and reached out and clung to him, tipped her face a trifle from him and held her face against his grimy shirt, rolling her forehead to and fro against his hard shoulder muscles.

Then all the starchy stiffness seemed to go out of her. She sagged down until she was seated on her bed, drawing him with her, and he twisted to half sit beside her, most of his weight uncomfortably borne on one braced leg. A wild thought pierced him, a remembrance of the dream he'd had about her one night; and as instantly as the thought came he was shamed by it, and another memory came unbidden, of a man he remembered from his boyhood, a lay preacher, a man riddled and twisted and wracked by his own wickedness, who backslid regularly and then was reconverted at the next meeting in a bathos of remorse and renunciation ... He remembered the time, one of the backslidden times, when the man, half-drunk and a-jitter with this spell of wickedness, leered and snickered and urgently confessed: 'Ah, that's the time, boys, and mark it down I know. Comfortin' a widder ... that's when ... specially she's a young widder, and full o' juice and the sorrow just a-oozin' ... Ah, boys, I'm tellin' you—I've slept mighty warm, a-comfortin' a widder ... seems that's when they're most missin' a lovin' man ... " Lanahan realized suddenly he hated that man—had always hated him. ... What the hell business did he have thinking of him? ... Dammit all anyway!

He felt no great sorrow at Prather's dying; his relationship with the man had been too impersonal and businesslike and their span of acquaintance too short for any real bond to have grown between them. He mourned the man abstractly, and was genuinely sorry for the girl's misery, and understood its terrible effect on her. Because her hurt was so deep he felt that hurt, and wanted somehow to help; he freed an arm and dragged a kerchief from his pocket and then realized he couldn't even offer that filthy thing, and he wadded it violently in his hand, working and kneading it because he was helpless to do anything with any action.

One of her hands groped and found his and held it tightly, and he desisted the kneading motion so that she would not think he was trying to draw away ... He thought again of that sinful leering backslider and cursed him violently and silently and felt the warmth of her thigh through her dress where she held his hand. His braced leg began to quiver from the awkward strain, and he felt the moist warmth of her sobbing breath against his breast. Her warmth and softness lay under his arm and leaned its weight against him; and the strain of warring impulses inside him was a thing of dismal weights and pressures and sharpnesses. And as suddenly as it began she ended it.

The great shuddering sobs broke off; she breathed deeply, shakily, her whole body moving to the effort of each breath, but she sobbed no more, and under his arm he could feel the gathering of strength, the slow regaining of control over muscles gone slack and soft. She rolled her forehead against him once more and drew back. She took her hand from his and reached into her sleeve for her own handkerchief. He drew back, half reluctantly and half in relief, and she scrubbed at her eyes, blew her nose vigorously.

She did not look at him. She said in a small hoarse voice, 'I don't know what came over me.' And then in a tone of near wonderment, 'That's the first time I've cried like that since he died.'

'Why,' he said soberly, 'I spect it's good you did. Likely it's worse to keep it bottled up.'

He got up from the bed, stood looking broodingly down at her. 'Anything I can do? You want me to send one of the boys ahead and try to catch Homer Flagg?'

'No,' she said. 'Thank you.'

Something in that stirred him, unconsciously, but he didn't stop to evaluate it. 'Whatever you say. I can have one of them drive you down to Fort Hall; likely you could make it on to Cheyenne all right. You got anybody, any friends, maybe, who...'

She looked at him. Her eyes were red-rimmed, swollen, her lips had a somehow bruised and gently swollen look, but her tone was firm. 'I am not going anywhere, Mr. Lanahan.'

'Why, I'm not trying to crowd you. I'll get out of here so you can rest, and you can take your time deciding...'

'I've already decided. I'll go on with the herd.'

He had turned half away, and he wheeled back, staring at her. 'With the herd? No. It's no place for a woman.'

'Ah,' she said not quite bitterly. 'No place for a woman. There's only one place for a woman, isn't there, Mr Lanahan?' She was blinking her reddened eyes rapidly, but she did not take her accusing look off him. 'Only one thing a woman's good for, isn't there?'

He said embarrassedly, 'Now, I'm not ... look here. I know you're all upset, and that's to be expected. I'll have Eben bring you something hot, and tomorrow...'

'I'm going on with the herd, Mr. Lanahan'

He looked down at her in bafflement. By God if he could figure a woman. A kitten one minute and clawing like a bobcat the next. With a mounting impatience he caught up his hat and slapped it against his leg.

'Be reasonable,' he said. 'Out here in the middle of nowhere, a bunch of men not used to having a woman around; you're not used to this life, and it would be just one thing after another. It ain't hardly a life for a white man, much less a woman.'

'You weren't born in a saddle, Mr. Lanahan. You've learned what you had to learn. I will learn what I must; do what I must. I'm aware that men have certain—functions; I won't be in their way. I expect they'll be gentlemanly enough to keep out of mine. Don't try to make a clinging vine out of me, Mr. Lanahan. I can be as tough as any man, if I must. And I have no choice. Neither do you. This is my herd, I am going with it. With your approval or without it.'

He raised his hat again, and then let the hand holding it fall to his side.

He said brusquely, matching her tone, 'I

can't drive you out of this camp, I suppose. But I can promise you one thing. You'll have your chance to show how tough you are, and once you start it'll be too late to change your mind. There's forty-odd miles of hell itself ahead, and no way of getting out of it. The herd's hurtin' some already, and they don't know what hurtin' is yet. Nor you don't either. But you sure as hell will before we get there.

'If that's the way you want it, so be it. But you'll have to cut your own swath and tough it out with the rest. I'm going to move out in an hour or so, if the cattle will move, and we'll be having no regular camps from now on. I can't spare anyone to look after you. If you need grub or water, see Eben. Keep your wagon out to the side, in the clear. I'll check with you whenever I get time. You say you're going to see this herd through. All right, that's the way it will have to be. I'll have to tend the herd, and you'll have to take care of yourself.' He turned away then, and left the wagon.

CHAPTER TWELVE

Lanahan descended the steps and walked around the wagon. A darker shadow detached itself from shadow and Tennessee's voice said, 'Now I thought this wagon was across the line to us common people. Or were you talkin' business all this while, boss man?'

For just a moment he was startled, almost embarrassed, and then the restrained impatience pushed through, and he said roughly, 'Are you adding standing in the dark and listening at windows to your accomplishments now? And what I do, my friend, isn't answerable to you or anybody like you.'

'You're sayin' now that the deadline's there for some an' not for others, is that it, boss man?'

'All right, for your information it's there. For you it's there, and for any other man in this outfit. You're over it now. Get back.'

He saw the dark shape of Tennessee stand in a quietness that was more threatening than violent motion. There was a silence of moments, and then Tennessee's soft, almost singing tenor. 'Say it plain, boss man. The line's there for me, but not for you.'

The challenge was there, and in Tennessee's stillness was readiness, and it was balm to Lanahan's scratches. He hadn't been able to fight grief, in the wagon yonder, for grief cannot be fought, it can only be endured. He could not loose impatience on yon strong-willed woman, for no matter how she flaunted her will, she was still a woman, and he could not do violence to a woman, no matter the provocation. But here was a man, crowding violence, almost insolently demanding violence, and inside Lanahan an urge rose to meet it. And in the same breath came self-control, for he could not yet let impatience free, nor drive it before him in frenzied flight.

He couldn't spare Tennessee. He did not think himself egotistical in that bald feeling. He searched himself in that infinitesimal fraction of time during which thought is born. He was not afraid of the man. Possibly he should be, but he was not. But he just could not spare Tennessee. Nor could he afford his enmity.

He said harshly, 'Her father is dead. She drove that damned rig all the way here, and she's beat down to nothing. I did what I could to help, and if that sticks in your craw, you spit it out whenever you're ready.'

The words had come spurting, but he'd known what he'd say before the words got out. He thought he knew how Tennessee would react.

'Ah,' said Tennessee, quietly, 'that's too bad. I had a hunch—when she came in. That's a dirty shame, boss man.'

Lanahan let his breath go, silently, sighingly. Tennessee hadn't even considered the harshness of tone. He hadn't backed down, nor had Lanahan; this hand was played, and there was no spilled-over rancor in awaiting the next one.

Lanahan said, still harshly, in the peremptory voice of a man too hard-pressed and abstracted to be particularly considerate, 'You can pass the word to the boys, Tennessee. She'll be with us the rest of the way, so let 'em know they'll have to watch themselves and not go to grasshoppering around when she's in sight. Now if those damned critters will move, I'm going to push 'em on tonight. I can't be everywhere at once, so I'm counting on you to do what you can.'

He could almost see Tennessee's thin grin in his voice. 'Now you mean, boss man, if there's anythin' you can't handle heah, I'm supposed to...'

Lanahan said wearily, 'God damn you, Tennessee, if I have to tell you again, I'll put a bullet through you and put an end to it. You tend to your job and not one goddamn thing else.'

'Just askin', boss man,' said Tennessee, letting a little of that grin still come through his voice so that it could be understood between them that it was just a joke now. 'Don't get your tail feathers up.'

'Aw, go to hell,' said Lanahan, because he knew Tennessee expected it, and it was in keeping with their conversation. He felt a trifle shamed, as if he'd tricked the man. A little later he wondered—Tennessee was nobody's fool. And a little later still, it made no difference at all, and was forgotten in the press of work. Have to remember, now, to send Beans or Jed back in the morning to hitch up a team for her. *Damn it all anyway. What'd she have to show up for, just now?*

* * *

Six miles that night. Seven, perhaps, the next day. The herd strung out in the harsh glare of day, the hot bake-oven wind holding the dust aloft, black gritty dust that moved with the herd, a great solid bank of dust, half a mile wide, miles long, towering up in writhing clouds from the shimmering earth.

The sound of the herd was sheer misery. The cattle moved with a sort of stupid inertia, as if moving were easier than the effort it would take to break the rhythm of their shuffling walk to stop. Their round onion eyes were dull and filmed, rimmed in blackened red, and like a herd of mechanical toys they grumbled at every few steps; not a healthy bawl of outrage or pain, but a simple automatic protest against the unknowable, grinding endless misery that was slowly driving life deep inside, into a smoldering compressed little ball of life that burned weaker and smaller with every hour.

No water that night and none the night

before. No water ahead, in nigh thirty miles. Nothing, save dust and heat and shimmering black rock and brush scrub so tough and desiccated that its green—or what should have been green—was almost black. Dust and heat and noise; that dull grinding miserable noise. No one rode the point, and only occasionally the flanks; hell, the whole damned herd was drags, it seemed. Then the drags bred stragglers, and a man could beat their bony rumps with a doubled catch rope till he was ashamed of himself, and they could not be hurried. Gradually they drifted and sifted, stringing along behind the slowest riders.

Here and there one would go down, perhaps from no more than one hoof stumbling over a rock no bigger than an apple; and when that one hoof buckled the animal went down and did not try to rise, and the others behind it might waveringly turn aside, or simply walk into that first inert body and sprawl half atop it. Then tiredly cursing men had to lean down from the saddle and haul up on the tail, wearily dismount and then tail 'em up, grunting and dangerously purple-faced from the effort expended in that rough succor.

The cavvy was far ahead, keeping out from under its own dust in better fashion; their want of water was not so great, and they were still foraging somewhat, tearing at the bone-dry grass clumps here and yonder. They were not suffering like the cow-brutes were because they'd been held at the last water; the mares and half of the geldings shuttled during the second night for another precious watering before they were brought up and past the herd, while every man traded horses.

The men dozed in their saddles, they dropped off over their beans and bacon when Eben stopped the chuck wagon for supper. They didn't really rest and they couldn't rest, for the herd never stopped, as a herd. Here and there a critter, or a pair, or a dozen, halted, stood spraddled, fell down incontinently, bawled even in their weariness and perhaps in their sleep. As the rest went on, some, the stronger ones, moved on, got up alone or were tailed up and so progressed, past still another group, down or halted in its turn. Through sunset's blessing, though the heat was but little diminished; through thick, furnace-heated dusk and early darkness; through later moonlight, which was a godsend. With a bit more cooling the breeze shifted, finally fell away, and the great dust cloud drifted aside, settled, slow as death. The moon laid a mantle of illusory beauty on utter starkness of rock and scrub and knobbed spine, touched gentle fingers on hat crown and brim edge and rein and cantle, the muscular rolling haunches of the slow walking mounts. The herd moved on.

Eileen had driven up during the night and halted her wagon about a hundred feet aside from the chuck wagon. Eben roughly insisted she share breakfast with the first shift of hands and, when all were finished, harnessed and hitched her team and his own. The curse of sunrise spread before them, and Lanahan, slowly drinking a last cup of coffee, saw her mount the rough little shelflike driving seat.

She wore a long-sleeved gown and soiled mitts and a slatted bonnet; her gown hung limp and loosely-fitted for she had dispensed with petticoats after the first day's broiling.

Eben tramped all the area around the fire, searching for any mislaid eating tools and said grouchily, 'You done with that cup yet?'

Lanahan drained it, tossed it to Eben, who rinsed it with a miserly trickle from the spigot of the barrel lashed on the chuck wagon sideboard, wiped it with a grimy rag and tossed it into a receptacle at the rear. He grunted and heaved up the broad tail gate and secured it, completely packed up now, and went to his own driving seat. Lanahan mounted, hesitated, then rode alongside Eileen Prather's wagon.

'How are you making out?'

She looked at him gravely and replied, 'I am all right. But those poor miserable creatures ... how much farther is it to water?'

He pulled up a corner of his mouth in an unconscious grimace and shook his head slightly. 'Twenty miles, or pretty close to it. It'll get worse before it gets better.' He looked at her closely. Her face was thinner; not haggard, but more closely cut in its shape. It was not unbecoming to her for she had a face of fine bone structure, and she was not gaunt or more unfeminine for the browning and thinning that the heat and stress had worked on her. Her wrists showed a dark angry red where the mitts and sleeves did not quite meet with her arms outstretched to the reins. The shelflike seat was narrow and uncomfortably pitched, but she rode it straight-backed and determinedly. Under this close scrutiny she made no sound or sign of complaint, and he touched his hat unconsciously and turned his horse away, angling back to clear the dust and send a searching look over the back trail for the telltale lumps and bulges that would mean downed cattle. He turned to follow the herd, pulled his kerchief up over nose and mouth as he entered the dust cloud, the damnable, irking, itching, turned-to-paste-with-sweat-then-baked-to-black-mortar-by-sun's-heat dust, fine as flour and lighter than ashes, supported by the slightest breeze and reluctant to fall. In that foggy eye-smarting haze he came on a downed one, stretched flat and birthing her calf; he pulled aside and little by little the dust went away, drifting with the herd on the following breeze, little by little falling from suspension in the air.

He pulled his masking kerchief down below his chin, hooked a leg around the saddle horn and rolled a smoke. It burned his lips, and seeped like acid into the deepest split in the center of his lower lip, pulled scales of dried skin off both lips when he took the paper cylinder from his mouth, and finally he crumpled it in discouragement and threw it into the dust. The cow groaned dismally in her labor. He sat broodingly watching the birth, as he had observed a thousand such, knowing how little chance this parturition had in the everyday miracle of creating a new life. He was right. The calf never got to its feet.

With dull patience he waited, giving the cow her chance, watched her nudging and licking and nuzzling the small thing. It tried twice and never really got its hind legs under it; dust caked on its wetness and its feeble breathing scarcely stirred the fine, black, floury stuff.

He dismounted finally, but the cow made a staggering charge and he had to dump her with his lariat and knew it was wasted effort by the time he laid a hand on the calf. It did not even struggle as he lifted it. He boosted it to his saddle, swung up behind it, threw a rippling hump running down his rope to loose the hondo so that the cow could kick out of the loop, and rode on to the calf wagon. There he got a rag wet with precious water and swabbed the tiny thing's nostrils and mouth, and knew he was going to a hell of a lot of trouble in a hopeless case. Then he went back and hazed the staggering cow to catch up with the rest.

That night, the third night, when the calf wagon was halted, there were three dead ones to be dragged in a bundle at the end of a catch rope far off to the side and left in a hollow in the ground; Lanahan did not check to see which had succumbed. The herd moved on.

It was more than flesh and blood could stand; but they stood it, most of them. Drags kept falling back, and here and there cattle went down and couldn't get up, wouldn't get up, wouldn't be tailed up or beaten into motion. With one step they were moving and on the next one they went down and to hell with it. Nothing to do but leave them. That night, the third night, the herd was strung out over a span of three miles, and now they were quieter; even the mechanical grumbling was lessened, and Lanahan felt a touch of foreboding. He rode ahead and found the marker he'd left on his exploratory ride to the river days before. He'd figured this marker at roughly fifteen miles. Say a couple of miles back to the leaders—he shook his head in near resignation. He rode back to the herd.

Eben was feeding the men, and Lanahan rode toward the Prather wagon, stark and dusty in the scorching sunset light, sent a rasping hail ahead in warning of his coming.

She came from around the wagon, walking with stiff tiredness, and abruptly he felt sorry for her. She saw who it was, and her shoulders lifted slightly. He wondered vaguely why that was, and then he swung down, dislodged dust from every crease and fold of his clothing, astonished that she could manage to look even passably neat out here.

Then he dropped that thought and said abruptly, 'I'm sending the cavvy on ahead, soon as we change horses. I'm taking the last of the water for the horses we'll ride tonight, and then Ebe will go on too, and you can go with him. If you think you can drive it, I'll have somebody hitch in a team for you in about an hour. If not, you can ride with Ebe and trailer your outfit behind the chuck wagon. If we're not there with the herd by tomorrow night we'll never get there, and if the horses don't get water tonight, we'll be afoot.'

'I can drive,' she said. 'But I hate to go. It seems wrong, somehow—those poor miserable things.'

'You can't do anything for them. There won't be any water. The hands will have a canteen of cold coffee, and that'll have to hold 'em till Eben gets back. So there's nothing for you to do but go with him.'

'All right,' she said. 'I have some water left.'

'Good, we can use it. Save enough to get you there, though. I'll send somebody in about an hour, then.'

He swung up into the saddle, and she tipped her head a trifle back to look at him.

'I saw you carrying a little calf on your saddle today,' she said. 'Is it all right?'

'Don't know. Haven't checked.'

'Then why did you bother with it, if it's no more important than that?'

He looked at her expressionlessly. 'If it lives, it's worth five dollars—in Wyoming.'

'Ah,' she said softly, 'still no gentleness then, Mr. Lanahan?'

He looked down at her again, then shook his head in the slightest of movements. 'Not enough to mention, Miss Prather,' he said evenly.

CHAPTER THIRTEEN

She watched him ride away from her, straight-shouldered but slack in the saddle, and she knew his tiredness; it had been in his eyes and his stance and his voice; and still he would not consciously show it before her, and she wondered why and in the same instant answered that question simply by knowing his pig-headed pride. If it weren't for that, she could almost be sorry for him, and knew too, as instantly as that thought came, that a single word of sympathy would stiffen his back like the bite of whip.

Ah, well, perhaps a man could afford pride; maybe because it was so precious they begrudged any of it to a woman ... Even her father, tired and sickly, driving himself at something in which he had little knowledge and little skill; somehow proudly, almost desperately withholding from her what he must have known long before—the fact that he was dying of cancer; leading her to believe, if not actually lying to her about it, that his illness was no more than the lingering ailments which had come as aftermath to his bout with pneumonia in Portland ... *Oh, Dad—why* ...

She clasped her hands together, welcoming the hurt of pressure on sunburned fingers while she slowly, carefully, with rigid control, forced that wild despairing wish back where it belonged.

Mister Lanahan, now. Mr. T. C. Lanahan. Terence Clairbonne Lanahan. *Most people call me Clay, Miss Prather* ...

Now why do you suppose that was? Did he think it a sissy name? Maybe, the way it went in most places with most men, they'd call him Terry. Probably he didn't like that. Terence was a nice name. Irish-sounding. Clairbonne sounded French. Terence Lanahan fitted together very well; how did that Clairbonne get in there? Was it his mother's name, d'you suppose? Family name, that is. *Well, now, missy, there's an end to this woolgathering.*

There's the clean syrup bucket; the lid will press tight enough and it will hold water enough for tonight, to drink, anyway; the very thought of water to wash with is sinful, thinking of how precious every drop will be to those horses and men who will be working ... And likely now, Clay Lanahan will be dryer than the rest, for it's in him, the way it was with Dad ... He'd be the last to drink and the last to rest ... when has he slept, anyway? If at all, it has been in the saddle, or nodding over his plate at mealtime. ... *And what concern of yours is that, pray tell, missy? Stop woolgathering and be getting ready. An hour he said, and an hour he meant, if I know Clay Lanahan....*

She thought then of Homer Flagg, wondered if he'd got any of the telegrams she'd sent ahead, not knowing when one might catch him; Virginia City would probably be the nearest; ah, well, he'd know there wasn't anything he could do...

He should be far beyond this place now—he'd not have embarked on any such ragtag and bobtail adventure. Homer, was a planner, an experienced cattleman, and he'd tried to tell her father; once, bluntly, came very near to calling him a fool to his face. Homer's big strong steers might have gone two nights without water on this stretch of hell, but not longer. She knew he had contracted for some twenty-five hundred of them, and had ten riders exclusive of his cook and horse wranglers; they'd have bunched those steers and come through here a-whooping—*My, my, missy, what strange words you pick up around a cattle herd...*

She found herself measuring the two men one against or beside, the other. Homer bulked larger; there was a bigness about him, in his body, in his thinking; he planned well and moved with authority; he knew what he wanted and went after it. Had she gotten snippety with him, he would simply have laughed at her, moved in to kiss her, given her a little roughly gentle shake with his big strong hands and told her to stick to her knitting and let him handle his work ... She'd never have touched his blunt pride, his sureness, with anything she said.

Clay Lanahan's lean height and quickness would seem almost slight beside Homer. There was a fire in him, never too deeply banked, something that wasn't quite nervousness or irritability, and also a coiled and ready resilience. You didn't move Homer—he was immovable, once he took a stand. Clay Lanahan gave a little when you pushed him—then snapped back, not only upright but beyond, in reaction to match the pushing force ... Her cheeks grew warm, thinking of a couple of times when she had gotten a trifle snippety—no, that wasn't really it, she'd thrust at him, not quite daring to admit she was testing him and not knowing quite why—and he had snapped back, but kept himself somehow under control while doing it, which in a way was more alarming than complete unrestraint ... *Ah, now, he's part of an unavoidable bargain—why do you do Homer the injustice of measuring them together?*

Suddenly she was tired, completely tired, and dreading the jolting and hammering of a long drive atop what she had already done that day. In that instant she longed for Homer to be there, big and strong and assured, to take her in hand and pass the quick sure orders that would fetch her cold water (somehow he'd manage that), give her darkness and cool blankets to sleep off her tiredness and someone to move the outfit smoothly and competently where she wanted it moved; perhaps take time to sit and talk to her, and assure her that everything would be all right—because he, Homer was going to see to it—and go on to sleep now and don't fret your pretty head about it for one moment, don't fret about how I'm going to do it because I'm going to take care of it—And quite suddenly she cried silently, *How? What would you do with two thousand staggering, dying, moaning creatures out here, without water, with little hope of reaching water; how would you do it, Homer—or anyone else?*

Abruptly she came out of those fantasies, knew they came from her own tiredness and worry, and knew also that no one was going to get her out of it, that all she could do was aid Clay Lanahan in the way she best could: by taking her own responsibility and care off his shoulders. Almost bustling about it, she drew her meager water ration, unshipped the light, almost empty keg from its stand, rolled it to the back door for whoever might come for it, and heard the boy Beans calling as he brought horses to hitch in for her.

The tough ones, the individualists, the leaders that had tramped out ahead now for their slow hundreds of miles, they smelled the water first, with nigh ten miles still to go. One of them, a rangy steer, slab-sided and hollow-tipped, raised his head suddenly, came out of his shambling trudge to walk almost alertly, and a low moaning sound came out of his lungs. Then another, and another, began to catch it, and a long shuddering ripple seemed to run through the immense sprawling body of the herd. Lanahan pulled out to the side, looking back; and Tennessee came, walking his mount slowly out of the pall of dust, to pull up alongside Lanahan.

He pulled the masking bandanna down from over his nose and mouth and sat slackly and silently. He raised his hand finally, gingerly explored his split lips with a filthy fingertip, and said, 'Boss man, I've made some mistakes in my time, but this caps them all. I'll never forgive you for catchin' me broke.'

'Never forgive myself if I hadn't,' said Lanahan almost absently. 'You've earned your pay.'

The herd crept by, stumbling, groaning, limping, dull-eyed skeleton cattle, slogging one weary hoof after the other, near dead in their misery, but moving...

* * *

Eben Longquist came out of the glaring sunrise. He had cleaned out the calf wagon and loaded every barrel, keg and bucket that would hold water. He pulled up as Lanahan approached, blinked red and puffy eyes and said resentfully to Lanahan, 'Well, here 'tis. What th' hell y'gonne do with ut?'

'I'm goin' to bring those damn down cows in with it,' retorted Lanahan. 'But I didn't mean you didn't have some sleep coming. Didn't figure you back before noon, anyway.'

Eben said discouragedly, 'Hell, don't you know more people die in bed than any place else?' He looked around at the others homing on the wagon, and demanded, 'Y'all et yet?'

'Sho,' said Tennessee. He stepped from his saddle directly onto the side of the wagon, thrust head and shoulders under the rolled-up canvas and dipped a cup into a bucket. 'I been eatin' sagebrush all night. After that bunch grass, it ain't bad.'

'Well, then, you won't want no breakfast,' said Eben. 'Quit hoggin' all that damn water. Think you're the only one got a dry on?'

He descended from the driving seat, went to the rear of the wagon, started dragging things out on the ground. 'Gimme elbow room,' he said testily, 'an' I'll have yer damn breakfast.'

Before their unbelieving eyes, he did it. He had bread sliced, and cold meat. He had a packet of ground coffee, and a quart of molasses. He had dry driftwood, hauled from the distant river bank, and within minutes, coffee was boiling pungently and the food laid out.

Bud Armishaw said happily, 'Eben, I take

back ever' mean thing I ever said about you. I hope you marry the fat lady and have six sets of twins.'

Eben growled, 'You're the sonofabitch told the boys I din' know how to boil guts fer a bear, remember? I ain't forgot it. Take that hunk o' meat, there; it looks big enough to match your mouth. Go on, choke, you damn pig.'

Tennessee said soberly, 'Eben, from now on you're muh pardner. I don't want you to borrow no money from nobody else, and I don't even want to see you out scratchin' around for wood. Don't you lift a hand. I'm youh friend, from this minute. I'll have Beans drag in eveh stick o' wood you burn from heah on in to Wyomin', an' that's a deathbed promise, sweah to God.'

Beans choked, swallowed, turned purple, spewed coffee that had started down the wrong way.

Tex Walker said, '*Don't* take that bitty stick to kill 'im with, Beans; grab that big 'un over there.'

Thus for the moment they forgot their tiredness and misery, and every man of them felt a gratitude he'd have died before stating aloud to the grouchy cook who'd gone sleepless and driven all night to give them this meal. Lanahan finished his hot, sweetened coffee and said, 'Remind me to raise your wages, Ebe, when I get time.'

‘Hell,’ said Eben, ‘you paid me what I’m worth, you couldn’t afford me.’

When they were finished, Lanahan said, ‘George, Bud, Tennessee, you’re in charge, go on with the herd. There’ll be no stopping them now, them that smell water. Split ’em in bunches and don’t let ’em pile up after all this. Tex, you come with me and Eben. Beans, you go with Tennessee. Let’s go.’

It was an hour’s ride back to the shambling weaklings of the drag. The great black dust cloud wavered up a full six miles long, and never were their ears quit of the nerve-twisting complaining of the animals.

Back behind the drag, that was the worst. Maybe fifty cows were down, back there, and these were the ones Lanahan was after. He swung down as he came to the first one, who lay with her nose almost in the dust, so that every breath stirred up a little black whirlpool. Her eyes were closed, and her tongue lolled, dry as leather. Lanahan tailed her up, roughly, for pain was just a dim memory to the animal now. At the third try, with Tex’s help, she came up, to stand with legs wide spread. Lanahan got a lard bucket of water and pulled it up over her muzzle. Her breath bubbled in it, and she snorted at it twice before she could remember to drink.

It was like new life. In mere seconds, her eyes opened to nearly full width, her gulping breathing eased.

'All right,' said Lanahan. He mounted again and the wagon trundled across the gritty earth.

Three more got water, but the fifth one could not be roused. Lanahan shook his head and slid the .44 out of its holster. The shot echoed down through the twisted alleys of lava, died out in the distance in a woodpecker rapping as the closing walls tossed the sound to and fro.

When they were done, twenty-odd head of cattle staggered after the wagon, following the wide scuffed trail of the herd. The kegs were all empty, and the barrel of Lanahan's pistol was too hot too touch comfortably.

They came out of the crest of the rocky reach down to the banks of the river—a scarecrow outfit, a wagon complaining and rattling its sun-dried spokes, riders grimy as coal miners, cattle staggering, moaning, muttering, three-quarters dead but still coming. Clay Lanahan swayed in his saddle, tired to the bone, the marrow, the innermost fibres of his body.

The chuck wagon was there on the bank, with water, precious, precious water, in uncounted tides and floods of gallons, running free alongside. Eileen's wagon parked close, and the unmistakable swing of a woman's skirt by the chuck wagon fire—and over across the river, a rider coming at a slow lope through the brush and rock, carrying his marking column of dust with him.

One of the boys has been out hunting, thought Lanahan without particular interest. Then his red eyes went back, caught the swing of wide shoulders, the tilt of the round-crowned hat, and recognition came.

It was Homer Flagg.

CHAPTER FOURTEEN

It wasn't pain, and it wasn't quite anger. It was more of a sense of complete tiredness; a feeling, somehow, of near defeat—which was senseless in itself, because this miserable little bunch of cattle were cattle saved from the dead. The precious few swallows of water that Lanahan had forced on them had made the difference between their staggering life and their inevitable death, back there in the lava.

Lanahan had known that. Another trail boss would have marked it off his book; for a down critter fifteen miles from water is dead without question. Only a fool would have tried it, only a bull-headed fool have carried it out. And somehow, suddenly, it wasn't important any more.

Lanahan took his eyes off the figure of Homer Flagg across the river, waved Tex and Eben ahead, and angled across the slope, quartering away from the wagons. He told himself that all he wanted was a long wallow in the water, but he knew that really he didn't want to see the meeting of Flagg and Eileen.

A thicket of willow grew down here on the bend and Lanahan came down stiffly out of the saddle, yanked loose the latigos, and dumped the heavy saddle on the ground. He had to pull the thirsty animal forcibly away from the water after a few gulps to keep it from foundering itself, and tie it to a slick-skinned trunk. Then he stripped his dust-caked clothing off and slid into the gentle turn of the shallow backwater.

The touch of the water was a silken caress. His leathery skin seemed to open up and soak in water like a sponge. In a sudden exuberance, he thrust his head clear under, took a mouthful of water, squirted it out between his teeth. He scrubbed his face harshly with rough hands, working his fingers deep into the roots of the wiry scrub of black beard he hadn't attempted to shave in a week. He raked clawed fingers through his hair, soused under again, came up to let the wonderful touch of water run down over his shoulders. Then he lay back, floating in two feet of water, completely limp, eyes closed, feeling his trailing fingers touch bottom once in a while as the almost imperceptible current turned him slowly. He sighed gently, in exquisite pleasure.

* * *

Eileen Prather stood in the shade of her wagon, still feeling the need to shade her eyes with both hands as she saw that last little staggering group of cattle brought in to water. Some of the main herd still stood, as if they would never get enough of the precious stuff, belly deep in the stream in knots and clumps and bunches; others were loosely flung out through the willows and in the green of watered grass, taking their first good feed in three days. She saw Lanahan's shape, the other rider, the wagon, and she thought to wave at them; but before the gesture was begun, she saw Lanahan turn his mount aside, to drop down an angled slope of the bank and out of sight at the upstream bend.

She turned back toward the fire then, with the blackened coffeepot on its crane; Tennessee was drinking a cup, and he lifted it as she turned toward him, in a sort of salute, and his teeth showed against his grimy face as he smiled.

She smiled back, feeling a strange comradeship for the man, for all of them, which no one would understand unless they had come through this last trial with them. She saw his glance lift above the cup as he sipped, and then he lowered the cup from his lips, sent a stare of something near accusation at her and quite deliberately turned half away.

She saw Homer Flagg then, riding a big sweating bay horse, splashing deep and hurriedly across the stream, moving the horse impatiently forward with his spurs as it hesitated momentarily at something underfoot in the fording place.

'Homer,' she cried, almost in unbelief, as he brought the horse splashing and surging up and onto the bank and directly toward her. 'Homer!'

He swung down out of the saddle and came to her, lifting his big arms to her, and he caught her and held her close, close and strong and comforting, saying, 'My dear. Eileen.' He bent his head to kiss her, and after only the slightest of hesitations, she responded, felt the sudden urgent gathering-in of her body against his. At the fire Tennessee dropped his cup with a tinny sound, wheeled, stalked to his mount and swung up, immediately moving off in the direction of the herd.

Homer said hungrily, close to her ear, 'I wasn't sure I would find you here, Eileen. It's good I didn't miss you; I came back from Virginia City as soon as I could.'

He released her and held her at arm's length and stared hungrily. She was glad she had had the chance to bathe in the stream; at dawn, after Eben had left her alone, to haul the water kegs back to Lanahan, she had half-guiltily but entirely pleasurably stripped off the dusty grimy clothing she had worn and run splashing into that cool water, tumbled and sprawled and reveled in it, scrubbing her hair and her skin, shamelessly exposing her nakedness to the touch of sun and air and water, a little drunk with the sense of complete privacy and the simple sensations of relief. She flushed hotly, thinking of that, thinking of what might have happened if Homer had come riding then without warning . . . She was suddenly aware of the heat in Homer, the strong male smell of him, the urgency in his tone and in his eyes. She drew back a trifle. 'I'm glad you are here,' she said.

Homer cocked his head a little, almost as if he were listening for something not quite apparent in her tone, and then smiled widely. 'So am I,' he said. Then, sobering, 'Though I'm sorry it had to be this way; because of your father, I mean.'

She took one deep breath, and said, 'It's all right, Homer. I've—had my cry out. It isn't so hard, any more.'

He said quietly, 'I wish you'd had my shoulder to cry on.'

She thought whose shoulder she had cried on, and sought to keep any of that thought from showing on her face and was aware of his close, almost searching regard. After a moment he said, still quietly, 'Ah, well, you'll have it from now on.'

'No,' she said, 'it is all over. I am not a weeping woman, Homer; I thought you would know that.'

'Why, yes,' he said, 'I thought I knew you, Eileen.' He let his hands drop to his sides.

'Now,' he said in a brisker voice, 'I don't want to rush you, but then there isn't any time to waste. I'll have one of your hands bring in a horse for you; it will only be a couple of days' riding; I know where there's a decent harness rig I can get...'

'But, Homer,' she said, 'I can't leave the herd now.'

His eyes left off the almost absent look of planning, and he said, 'Nonsense. What can you do? Not one thing, except spend another miserable month on the trail, and that I won't hear of. No, we'll push on to Virginia City; we can be married there, and I'm sorry it can't be as fine an affair as I'd planned for you—but I'll make up for it to you. I can get things squared away at the ranch in short order—we can go on the steam cars from Cheyenne anywhere you want to go, for your wedding trip. Ah, the bad times won't even be a memory, Eileen.'

She said in a sense of near desperation, 'I can't, Homer. I just can't. It's like throwing away everything Dad has done; can't you see that, Homer?'

He stood so close she had to tip her head back to see his face. 'No,' he said bluntly, 'I don't see. I don't see any of it except you. I never wanted any woman the way I want you. God knows I've had my pick of others'—she saw his face as he said that, and there was no trace of conscious conceit in his face or his voice—'... but you are the only one. If I speak too plainly, too bluntly, it is because that is the kind of man I am. You are the only woman for me. You accepted, when I offered. I don't intend to take second place with you for anything...'

She said swiftly, 'You aren't second in...'

'Let me finish,' he said. 'I held back for your father. I was disappointed, but I held off, thinking that sometimes first things come first. But your father is dead—dead and gone—and your reasons for holding back from me are gone. I could respect your mourning him, Eileen—but I'll not play second fiddle to anything else. I tell you, Eileen, I won't permit anything to stand between us. Maybe I talk too plain, but I'm a plain man—and I think I've waited long enough.'

'Why,' she said, showing the lift of her own spirit, 'you don't own me, Homer Flagg. Don't you ever think you'll lay down your word for me to follow like holy law.

Don't tell me what you'll have or won't have. Yes I accepted you, because you acted like a man who knew his mind—because you didn't simper and flatter me or offer yourself like a rag rug. Well, I'm not either, and don't you ever forget it. When I come to you it will be of my own free will and without holding anything back or bargaining. But you won't order me around like a hired hand or something you own. And that you can very well chew over, mister-big-man-on-your-high-horse!'

For a moment he looked at her with a deep and deadly seriousness; then slowly a tight reluctant smile spread on his lips. 'Ah, Eileen,' he said quietly, 'I'm not a man to bow my neck for any man's yoke—or any woman's. I think that is why you are the one for me. I wouldn't want you without that spirit. Just take care it doesn't hurt you. My way doesn't go all around Robin Hood's barn. Ah, Eileen, why are we fighting this way? What is it that has gone wrong? It wasn't like this before with us.'

She said, meaning it, 'I don't know, Homer. I think—if you had been there—when Dad—died—I think then I ... Oh, I don't know. It is just something I *must* do, Homer. Something tells me I must finish what I have begun. If I went with you now I would feel wrong. I don't want it to be that way, believe me, Homer.'

He looked down at her in bafflement. Slowly his smile faded, and a closed, brooding look came on him. He breathed deeply, held that breath, let it go in a slow sighing sound. Almost distantly he said, 'Think on it. Maybe I have come at you too quickly. Think on it. I'll be back soon.' He gave her a small brief smile and turned away, caught up the training rein of his waiting horse and mounted. 'Everyone with the herd?' he inquired casually.

She looked around. Tennessee was gone; but Eben worked at his chuck wagon, carefully not glancing their way. 'I think most of them are,' she said. 'All but Clay ... Lanahan. I saw him up that way, just a while ago.'

He looked down at her, his expression distant and unreadable. 'Ah, yes,' he said, 'Clay Lanahan.' Then he pulled his big bay mount about and rode on upstream.

She watched him, feeling a peculiar jumble of emotions. Finally she turned toward where Eben worked.

'Eben,' she called. 'Can't I help you with something?'

Eben gave her a look midway between outrage and surprise. 'No, ma'am,' he growled emphatically. 'I'll do what needs did.'

* * *

Lanahan finally, reluctantly, heaved himself up and out of the water, waded ashore, shivering a little unconscious shiver as the wind touched his wetness, stripped water off his flat lean belly with the edges of his hands, and regarded the dirty pile of clothing with distaste.

He compromised by beating dust out of his trousers with a willow limb before he pulled them on, then squatted down on the bank, barebacked and barefooted, and soused his filthy shirt in the cool clear water. He dipped and squeezed, dipped and squeezed, watching the little dark filaments of muddy water writhe off and disperse in the clear running water of the stream, scrubbed the heavy bundle between his double fists. Above that sound he heard the horse coming, and looked over his shoulder as Homer Flagg rode in close, sat for just a moment, and then dismounted.

'See you made it,' Flagg said.

Lanahan gave him a brief glance, looked back at his shirt and said shortly, 'Yes.'

'Lose many?'

'Some. Haven't tallied.'

Flagg stood, bulking up against the sky, wide and confident, eyes closely evaluating Lanahan.

'Lucky,' he said. And then, very casually, 'Where did Miss Prather catch up with you?'

Lanahan flicked a quick look and said, 'Around that mud pond, past the lava beds. Why?'

'Just wondering. And I'm wondering why she insists on sticking with the herd.' Lanahan rocked back on his bare heels and stood up. He looked at Flagg with full attention. Then Flagg went on almost musingly, 'You Texans must have a way with women. I wonder how much of it is her own idea.'

Lanahan whipped him across the face with the water-heavy wool shirt, letting the black temper inside him go, in a full-armed swing that made the sodden shirt hit Flagg's face like a length of board. Flagg staggered sideways, one heel slid in the mud of the bank, and he pinwheeled over on his side into the water with a flailing splash.

Lanahan took a wheeling step away, stooped, came up with a whisper of leather as his gun slid out of the holster atop his piled clothing. He eared the hammer back to full cock and braced his wrist against his hip.

Flagg's hand made a little splash, stopped in its motion as the round black muzzle of Lanahan's gun frowned dismally upon him.

Lanahan said through his teeth, 'Go ahead, draw.' Flagg pulled himself over to a sitting position in the shallow water and looked up, unwinking, without change in expression, without speaking. Lanahan waited a second, saw that Flagg was not going to move.

'God damn you, Flagg,' said Lanahan. 'Damn you and your big mouth. You talk like you're the he coon around here. You act like the whole damn world spins around the spot you happen to stand. Now you come mouthin' around me about your damned woman. Sniffin' around like a yellah dog at a garbage pit, seein' if you can smell somethin'. Why, God damn you, if I had taken your woman, you think I'd tell you? If you're bracin' me, why don't you brace me with a gun in your hand? You know what I think you are? You're a big bag of wind with a mouth at one end and a blowhole at the other!'

Flagg's eyes were staring and shiny, and his voice came thick and rough. 'You're pretty brave, holding me under the gun.'

'Damn right I'm brave. You think the world revolves around you and what you want. Well, it don't mister, and just because you think so don't mean I play the game the way you want. Just this once, you big-mouth sonofabitch, you're goin' to do things my way. Just because I'm the big he coon right now. You make one move for that gun and I'll blow your stinkin' brains right on out of the back of your head.'

Flagg took it. His face contorted under the lash of Lanahan's words, but he took it. And then slowly, very slowly, his features moved into an expression that showed nothing at all.

'Fine,' said Lanahan. 'Now you've got it. When I let you out of here, you're going to go right on out through my camp, and from there on, you are going to keep going. You can take her with you, or not, just as you please. That's up to you and it's up to her. But either way, you keep going. And the next time you see me, you step aside, or make your fight, or I'm goin' to walk right over you. Just because I've got an absolutely complete bellyful of you. Now haul your butt out of there.'

Flagg said nothing, did nothing. His face was as carefully expressionless as a block of wood. At the upward commanding jerk of Lanahan's gun, he got up out of the water without haste, and took two splashing steps to the bank. He stopped, with the barrel of the gun not two feet from his belly, and he looked carefully at Lanahan—a slow, precise scanning of every feature. His voice betrayed him only in its curious thickness.

'You made a mistake, Lanahan,' he said. 'You'll pay for it.' It wasn't a threat. There was no heat to the words. It was a simple statement that cut through the man's impassive exterior and showed the adamant granite within, the positive bull force of the man.

Then he turned away toward his horse, moving easily, completely ignoring Lanahan's presence, and stooping to press some of the water out of his sodden pants. This done, he swung into his saddle, rode straight away without a glance back.

* * *

Eileen Prather unpinned a muslin wrapper, shook out the dress it enclosed.

She started and turned, at a heavy pounding at the rear of the wagon. It was Homer, sitting his horse, so that his head was almost level with hers as she stood in the doorway.

'Eileen,' he said without preliminaries, 'are you coming with me?'

She looked at him sharply, trying to decipher his tone, and seeing nothing, she gave him a little smile and said gently, 'I thought we had decided that, Homer.'

'We decided nothing,' he retorted bluntly. 'You decided.' His eyes were on her, cool and unreadable. 'I got manhandled a minute ago,' he went on in the same neutral tone, 'for asking a question. Maybe you'll give me the answer. What does this man Lanahan mean to you?'

She felt the blood draining from her hot face, and she asked in a voice that was little more than a whisper, 'You and Lanahan fought?'

'It was no fight. He knocked me down and threw a gun on me. What does he mean to you?'

She saw his face, cool, composed, showing nothing save for a slight lifting flare to his nostrils, a faint compression of flesh at the corners of his full lips that showed in two pale lines like pencil marks.

She saw those two danger signals, and she said steadily, 'He means nothing to me, Homer, except as the man who is working for me. No, I'll take that back. He has done more than wages could buy. He went back into that stretch of hell, yonder, without a drink, without a bite to eat, when he hadn't really slept in two days, and he brought out cattle that couldn't be saved. It will be hard to pay for that kind of loyalty with money.'

A little spark showed in Homer Flagg's cool eyes. 'So he'll get his pay another way,' he said.

Eileen's eyes blazed. 'If that's what you said to Lanahan,' she cried, 'I wonder he didn't kill you. If that is the way your mind works ...' She stared at him for a long moment, feeling a trembling inside that was neither hot nor cold, feeling an ebbing and flowing of anger that painted two fiery spots high on her cheeks. Then she said carefully, 'Homer, if I really believed you meant what you just said, I'd call the crew to drive you out of camp with a horsewhip. And I think the best thing for you to do is get out of my sight until I decide whether I ever want to see you again!'

The expression on Homer's face was as shocking as a blow. For in that moment a devil looked out of his eyes, in a gaze of pure fury, though his stiffly controlled features did not noticeably change. Then, slowly, that stiffness broke. As she finished, a smile came on him, a tight stretching of his full lips, a narrow shine of white teeth against his sunburned hide.

'Spitfire,' he said—admiringly, mockingly, wonderingly—she could not tell. 'I'm striking fire everywhere I go today. All right, Eileen. You haven't found the end of my patience yet. I'll go. But don't say good-by—don't even think it. I'll be back. I promise you, I'll be back.'

He studied her face just a moment longer, letting the smile fade to a more brooding expression, and then he hauled his horse around and lifted it into a lunging run with his spurs.

A moment later she heard the splashing as he took the ford. She felt herself shaking with a queer, undefined emotion that was neither anger nor fear. She snatched up one of the dresses, shook it violently.

So they'd fought. The fools—the crazy fools—since the first time they'd met, they'd...

No fight, Homer had said. *Knocked me down, threw a gun on me* ... Lanahan? She had seen the violence in him; a lean strength greater than his size. *But Homer? Knock down a tree, say, or a mountain—but not Homer*. She found herself half unbelieving, brushing at the dress with stiff mechanical fingers.

* * *

Slowly the heat went out of Clay Lanahan, and there came an abrupt letdown of reaction. His fingers were near to shaking as Homer Flagg went out of his sight and hearing. He shoved the .44 back into his holster, and had an odd desire to sit down and rest. He compromised by squatting on his bare heels, rooting out his tobacco and papers and rolling a smoke and lighting it. When it was down to a hot and stained little stub in his fingers, he tossed it into the water, picked his shirt up out of the dirt where it had fallen, washed it again, and threw it across a willow to dry.

The fierce fighting urge was gone from him, and he felt a touch of wonderment at his violence of minutes ago. He assessed his provocations as honestly as he could, looked critically at his reactions toward Flagg, and found no clearcut causation. The man simply was repugnant to him; rubbed him the wrong way; they clashed as simply and openly as two vicious fighting cocks every time they met.

Hell with it. He's an arrogant sonofabitch, and likely the next time you meet him you'll have to kill him and to hell with why. It's just the way it is. And in the next moment: *Wonder if he took her with him.* In the next moment: *All right, and if he did—what of it—she's his woman, and it's no skin off your butt. A load off your back, if anything.*

And in the end, he pulled on his boots without socks, tucked the still damp tails of his shirt into his pants, and rode back into the camp.

Eben was laboring at his fire, the herd was scattered to hell and gone down the bank, the door to her wagon was open—she came out and looked toward him as he rode in. Unconsciously his eyes searched and swept the campsite for sign or sight of Homer Flagg's mount; unconsciously his inner right forearm moved to locate the butt of the holstered revolver. She raised a hand to him and he veered toward the wagon.

Her smile had an oddly strained look to it, her eyes looked into his and away, her voice was almost natural as she said, 'Have a good swim?'

He said neutrally, 'Yes. I thought maybe you'd be gone.'

Her smile faded, and she looked at him

almost searchingly. 'No,' she said. 'I'm going on with the herd.'

He could not read her expression. Finally he lifted his shoulders in the slightest of motions, touched his hat and rode on.

He found half the crew sprawled in the shade and the rest splashing in the water, and he sat watching them a while before he grinned wryly and said, 'All right, out of the wallow and into your saddles. Holiday's over for now. Gather 'em up and shove on across. Let 'em loose on that bunch grass. Likely have half of 'em down and bloated on this green stuff if we don't. Come on out of there, you bathin' beauties, you've got to learn someday that trailin' cows ain't all fun.'

He ignored their bitter curses and dodged their flung mudballs, and portioned out their work. He was the last one in at the chuck wagon, and the only sign of life in Eileen's wagon was the yellow lamp-glow inside.

CHAPTER FIFTEEN

Through the Pass, in the clean sharp pine-smelling air; over a mile high, somebody said; but the incline was gentle, and the herd moved briskly, in its own way. Three day's rest and good feed had made a world of difference in the herd.

Yi-yi-yi-yi! What for you laggin' back here for, you gristly brute? Git along, there! You never had it so good, damn you. Git along!

Hoooooo-haaaa-a-ah! Virginia City ahead. What you gonna do the first thing, Tex?

None ah yer damn business. Tell yah the second thing I'm gonna do though . . . Watch it—these cow-brutes has got a delicate nature . . . Hey, Beans—you gonna side me inta the big city—sho, you are—you gonna bird-dog fer me, ain'tcha? Nah you don't, Bud. Beans is my toll dog. Why, them girls get a look at his innocent blushin' face an' they'll come flockin' like pahtridge, right inta my trap. Ain't that the way we got it fixed, Beans? You toll 'em in an' I trap 'em, and I'm bound to save a nice juicy one just fer you . . . Beans, what makes yore neck so red, boy?

She sure-to-God wasn't no metropolis. But she wasn't no cow camp nuther. She had big yellow lights a-blinkin' and glass in her windows and solid brass spittoons and girls with tight dresses and loose manners and whisky served in glasses and lilac water in bottles in the tonsorial parlors and God-only-knew-what-all. Why, a man might even get to see the elephant.

Gleefully, they rang all the changes on that one and, save the disappointed ones with night herd, they descended on the town.

Lanahan rode easy in the saddle, and unconsciously his eyes watched right and left. After a while he realized what he was looking for and not seeing, and wryly he laughed at himself; and after that did not knowingly at least look out for sign of a Flag-branded horse, or the loom of wide shoulders in the crowd.

Eileen Prather rode with him. As in Baker City, he saw her alert interest in everything about them, her expression of bemusement at the sights and sounds, a further expression that might almost have been wistfulness. She caught him watching her, turned a quick smile on him and said, 'New faces, new places, new things to see—do men enjoy them too?'

He said dryly, knowing what the men were seeing and thinking, 'I imagine so. The town looks busy; likely we've hit it at a bad time, being a Saturday. May have a time finding you a room.'

'I don't care what it's like,' she said. 'I just want a place to stay that is bigger than that wagon.'

'I'll see what I can do,' he said.

The second place he tried had a room for a lady; Lanahan went down the hallway with her, put the portmanteau on the floor inside the room and said, 'Brace that chair at the door tonight; looks like any key in the place would get in here.'

'All right,' she said. She took off her hat and looked around the room: bare walls painted, but not recently; the hanging lamp; the single small window that looked out on a shed roof across an alleyway. It was a rough room, a cheerless room, with a bed, a chair, a commode, a freckled mirror perhaps eight inches square. It was little better and no worse than most such out-country hotel rooms, a product of its times and circumstances; for though Virginia City was nearly a generation established, it was still a frontier mining town, and its roughness had been diminished only by the casual rubbing of many passing shoulders. But it was not a cheerful room.

Lanahan watched her eyes take it in, and on sudden impulse said, 'I'll take you to supper, after a bit. Will an hour give you time enough?'

She gave him a quick little smile and said, 'Thank you. But you don't have to take care of me. I'll be all right.'

'Haven't got anything else to do,' he said, and then had the grace to grin at the tactless sound of that. 'I mean, I'd enjoy taking you to supper more than anything else I've seen in this town. The dining room would be full of strangers, and it's a rough town.'

'All right,' she said. 'An hour, then, if it isn't rushing you.'

He found a barber's shop and found Jed in the first chair, his face red from the covering cloth's constriction on his weathered neck, with a barber snipping at his lank gray hair.

Lanahan took a seat and said gently gibing, 'This the *first* thing you're doin', Jed?'

'Just settin' an' simmerin' an' bidin' my time.'

Lanahan laughed at him. 'Your powder's damp now, Pop. You simmer another twenty minutes, and it'll be more of a fizzle than a bang.'

'You go to hell,' said Jed.

'Next,' said the barber, from the next chair.

Lanahan took the chair and said to Jed, 'Seen any of the other boys around?'

'Tennessee an' Beans hit some deadfall up the street; dunno where Ebe went. I'll buy you one when you're through; might even buy you two, you quit insultin' me.'

'Just one,' said Lanahan. 'I'm having supper with a lady.'

Jed let out a raucous bray, then shot a quick sidelong look at Lanahan and said, 'Oh.' Lanahan grinned faintly and tipped his head forward at the barber's behest.

He had that one drink with Jed, felt his facial skin all stiff and tender from the barber's close razoring, sniffed a little at his own fragrance of bay rum and whatever it was the man had combed into his hair. He got the money deposited at Wells Fargo, and then went on, looking the town over with the attention of a man long separated from people in bunches and herds.

Twenty years had sprouted a few brick buildings, laid walkways enough to keep foot traffic out of the mud along the main streets at least, and city dress was as common as riders' rigs and miners' rough working outfits. But she was no tame town, for on Saturday evening the streets were awash with traffic, and the crowding saloons and stores were busy. There was a steady, half-shouting urgency of sound, and at least once somebody fired off a shot down street without making any noticeable dent in the furor as result. He finished his cigar and went to the hotel.

At the doorway to the dining room adjacent to the lobby, he said to Eileen, 'I didn't see anything that looked any better than this, and most of them are busier. I guess we stand as good a chance eating here as anywhere.'

'This will be fine,' she said. She looked around the room with two long common tables and the few smaller ones at the sides. She murmured, 'Could we get one of the small ones, by the window? We could see something besides other people eating.'

A waiter came to their table shortly and said, 'We got beefsteak, beef stew, 'taters, green beans and stewed prunes.'

Lanahan considered, looking at Eileen and said, 'Steak for me. And potatoes and prunes. What would you like?'

'I'll have steak too. And the green beans, please.' She looked at Lanahan. 'I'd think you'd want green things after all that meat and bread and dried beans.'

'Ah,' he said carelessly, 'green stuff's for cows ...' Then he felt himself flushing violently and blurted, 'Now, I didn't mean it like ...' and then grinned shamefacedly when he saw she was laughing at his discomfiture. The waiter said stolidly, 'They ain't bad. Cook boils 'em with bacon.'

'I'll have that,' said Eileen.

'You too, mister?' said the waiter.

Lanahan said, still red-faced, 'I suppose I'll have to, now. But I want the spuds, too.'

'They'll be good for you,' said Eileen comfortably.

'Well,' murmured Lanahan, 'they can't be any worse than my foot in my mouth.'

He saw her bite her lip, and could not help but laugh himself, and he felt suddenly more at ease with her. When his steak came he ate with good appetite.

She said suddenly, 'How did you like the green beans?'

'Why, good,' he said, not quite blankly, 'I ...' He noticed then that he had eaten them without noticing, and really didn't know what they'd tasted like. 'It must be the company,' he said dryly. 'They tasted fine.'

Her quick interested look came on him

and she murmured, 'Mr Lanahan, you are becoming positively gallant.'

He flushed and said still dryly, 'Ah, my bark is worse than my bite.'

'I'm beginning to believe it,' she said. They ate the last of the sweet stewed prunes and finished their coffee. At her indication that she was finished, he stepped around to help her with her chair.

'Thank you,' she said. 'I enjoyed it. I was rather dreading eating alone.'

The words came without particular volition, 'How about breakfast, then?'

'Thank you,' she said. 'If you'll be—free.'

'Why not?' he said. He paid the waiter, took Eileen's arm without thinking as they were almost caught in a group entering the dining room against them.

'Like to take a walk?' he found himself saying. And then, almost abashed at himself for making the suggestion, 'Be too dark to see much pretty soon, though,' apologetically.

He felt better instantly at her quick delighted look. 'I'd like to,' she said. She took his arm as they went into the street, and strolled to the corner, where he took a quick evaluating look to see what sort of houses might be here; the fronts seemed prosaic enough and no beckoning lights burned, so they turned there and walked that street, companionably quiet.

She said once, in her decided tone, 'Eben is a better cook, if he had the things to do with.'

He said, 'That steak was all right, but I can pretty near tell to the mile how far it hoofed it from Oregon.' Idle talk, without thought or profundity, slow idling stroll, without aim or destination, her arm warm on his, but no hurtful ache of urgency; he was content, and felt her to be, and it was a time of simple pleasantness to him.

Idly he thought of how few such times he could remember; his life since childhood had been a thing of travel—with a place to go, a distance to be attained, but no really different thing there when he arrived; of jobs to be done, with rest enforced by the tiredness mauled deep by the job; this latter-day planning and responsibility, from the time he and Jed had come on the idea of breaking free of other men's jobs to and through this last duty with its weights and pressures and frustrations; the good times he remembered were mainly lonely times.

A hunting trip once, when he'd siwashed it for a week with a horse and all his outfit in a small pack behind the saddle; an aimless time in a lovely country of trees and streams where he shot grouse and caught fish, and no more than he needed to eat of either; the long lazy evenings with an aromatic pine-branch fire and a pleasant late chill that brought out all the warmth of comfort of his blankets, and without bitterness to rob the mornings of their sunrise glory. The screaming bugle of a bull elk in that crisp dawn, so that he felt his chest swell in an unconscious desire to send his own challenge back; the timid movement of deer in a thicket almost near enough to touch, the busy scamper of a striped chipmunk bestirring himself at his immediate task of searching for pine nuts. He had a sudden, simple, rather foolish wish that he could tell Eileen Prather about that, tell it well enough so she could see it; maybe—the thought discarded almost as fast as it came—*let* her see it, take her where that good time had been ... *Ah, man you're dreaming like a fool; you've got your belly full and a night out of the camp, and doing no more than the simple courtesy of lending your presence to another man's woman who'd be bottled up in a dreary room without a man—anything cut in shape of a man—as protector and escort...*

'Dark,' he said, stating the obvious because suddenly he wondered how long that last silence had lasted.

'Yes,' she said, and her agreement sounded reluctant. 'Nothing much to see—for a woman, at least.'

'Not much for anybody to see,' he said. 'It's a rough town. I've seen a hundred like it, and there is nothing in any of them except the few supplies you have to get—to go on to the next one. Or maybe it's just that I'm not a town man.'

He escorted her to her door, waited while she unlocked. He started to turn away then, and she said, looking up at him, 'What will you do now?'

He said, in a little discomfort 'Ah, not much. Likely look up some of the boys, have a drink or two, find a place to sleep.'

He could not read her slight smile. The light from the one lamp in the hallway was pale. 'Once I'm locked in,' she said almost wistfully, 'then you will be seeing things, doing things, that I wouldn't be permitted to see or do.'

'You're missing nothing,' he said. 'You wouldn't like a saloon if you could go there. There wouldn't be a thing you'd see or enjoy. There's nothing pretty about a bunch of rough men in a rough town.'

She looked at him speculatively. 'Why don't men want women to see their fun?' she said. 'I mean, their wives, their daughters, their sweethearts. There are women in some of those places, aren't there?'

He felt the furiously red flush sweeping over him, and was glad for the dim lighting in the hallway. He cleared his throat so as to be sure of his voice, and said it as calmly as he could. 'Some places,' he admitted. 'Other places are just—saloons. If you did walk in there, every man in the place would take his hat off, and not one man would say one word, good or bad, while you were there. It's no more than a place where a lone man can meet and talk with his friends and have a drink if he feels like it. It's no great fun.'

'Ah,' she murmured, 'you mentioned the lone men. Now Dad used to walk down a place in Portland; I know many married men did, for he'd mention he'd seen so-and-so tonight. What about that?'

Suddenly her determination to make something of it became a little funny to him, and he said dryly, 'It's also a place where a married man or a father can get away from women for a while. And they have a drink to numb the place where the feathers are going to be pulled when they get home. Don't forget to brace that chair-back to your door now.'

He grinned faintly at her suddenly surprised look, touched his hat, walked down the hallway, and heard her call softly, 'Clay ... Mr. Lanahan.'

He turned, saw her still standing, went back. 'I didn't mean to pry,' she said. 'I wanted ... to know. I couldn't—as you said—walk in and see for myself. I guess I was asking for—your last remark. And thank you. You have been very kind, to allow me to impose on your company.'

Impulsively, she rose on tiptoes, kissed

him softly and fleetingly at the corner of his mouth. Without thought or volition his arms caught her, brought her to him, and he kissed her, not fleetingly but earnestly, deeply, hungrily, feeling the softness and warmth of her all the length of his body as his arms tightened in a primitive and urgent reaction. Then he heard her soft sound of fright or pain, and he released her quickly, suddenly shaken and full of tension and dissatisfaction, but somewhat in control of it now, and he said in a harsh murmur, 'I'm sorry—no, damned if I am. You're the one wanted to know what men are like.'

She stood just a little back, still looking up at him; he thought her color was higher than before, but he could not tell whether her slight smile showed embarrassment or amusement. She moved through her doorway, turned, said softly, 'I'm the one to be sorry. I started it.' He thought her smile came richer then, fuller, and was almost certain of her amusement. 'At least,' she murmured, 'I know you're not as cold as you seem sometimes.' Then the door went shut in his face, though he heard no sound of the chair being drawn up to bolster it. He stood a moment, feeling fully roused and half silly, and then he wheeled and tramped down the hallway, letting her hear his departing steps. He went out through the lobby and into the street, moving restlessly, undirected, still with a feeling of confusion.

He cruised the street, saw no sign of Jed, did finally see Tennessee sitting in on a card game in one of the deadfalls. He stopped and watched a moment until Tennessee looked up and said, 'Well, boss man. Goin' to set in on a few hands?'

'Not now,' said Lanahan. He went to the bar and ordered a drink, saw down the length of the polished wood that Beans Riordan was being taken in tow by a brassy blonde, and that Beans was about halfway between discomfort and elation; grinned faintly and raised his own drink in sardonic toast to youth and innocence.

'You gonna buy me a drink, honey?' said a woman from beside him.

'Why not?' he said. He signaled the bar man and got the bottle, looked around to locate a table, saw two girls spot him and get up to leave the table where they had been sitting alone. 'Need another glass,' he said to the bar man.

'He'll bring mine,' said the woman who had accosted him.

'I know,' he said, 'full of tea. Tans your stomach, somebody told me once.'

'Now you don't need to go insulting the color of my stomach,' the girl said. He looked at her for the first time. She was small and dark and had an alert and wise little monkey face which was curiously appealing, despite its heavy makeup.

'Why don't you wash that stuff off?' he said. 'Looks like hell.'

'Cause we'd just look like girls then, and we wouldn't get enough business to buy a pair of stockings in a month,' she said impudently. 'You see the paint, you know you're gonna pay; wash it off and we look like any other girl, and you'll spend the night trying to talk us out of it.'

'Out of what?' he said grinning. The first drink was gone without a trace, and the second was warming him.

'Out of a meal ticket,' she said, and grinned back. 'You have to work for a living too, don't you, honey?'

'That I do,' he said. 'It's tough. You want to hear the story of my life?'

'No,' she said, 'and it'll cost you to hear mine.'

'Have a drink,' he said. She smiled and signaled toward the bar, and in a moment a waiter brought a little shotglass of amber fluid, ostentatiously made a pencil mark on a card, and went away.

'Tea,' said Lanahan disparagingly, and poured himself another drink.

'You're taking that pretty fast, ain't you, honey?'

He grinned, 'I don't give a damn *what* my belly looks like.'

She made a face at him. 'You wanna

dance, honey?'

'Nope.'

'You wanna ...' She lifted her eyebrows and delicately indicated the stairway at the rear of the room.

He looked at her carefully. He saw her very clearly—as if the whisky he'd downed so quickly had become a clarifying lens.

He said suddenly, 'What's your name?'

Something in his tone brought her attention sharply on him. 'Delia.' She smiled her wise puckish smile. 'Most people call me Deedee.'

'All right, Deedee; would you remember my face tomorrow?'

She said lushly, rapturously, leaning forward so that her bodice gaped close to his face, 'I'd never forget you, honey; don't you ever worry about that.'

'I'm not worried about that. What bothers me is that I'd remember you. And that's no good.'

'Well, damn you too,' she said.

'Forget I said that,' he said. He leaned back, and saw Beans, flushed, but still uncomfortable, at a table with the blonde. 'Look,' said Lanahan. 'See that kid back there—with the blonde?'

'Sure. That's Beatrice. High-toned name, ain't it? She's a bitch.'

'She looks it. All right.' He dug into a pocket, fumblingly, feeling suddenly the drinks he'd taken. 'Here. That's a good kid. He's on my crew. You go back there and take him away from her. Treat him right and keep him with you and don't let anybody roll him.'

She looked at him with her wise monkey look, then said, 'I'd be a pleasure, just to fix up Breatrice. But why me?'

He looked at her. 'He's going to remember a face, and I'd rather it would be yours than hers, that's all. Here's your money. Just get back in time to work tomorrow.'

She probed at him with her eyes, and then grinned suddenly and stood up. 'Sucker,' she said. Then she looked more closely at Beans, across the room. 'He's just a kid,' she said.

'You're not much older,' he said.

She laughed at him then. 'To hell with you,' she said. 'You had your chance.' She moved away with an exaggerated saunter that set her hips rolling under her tight dress. Lanahan could not see what happened, but the blonde looked up angrily and said something when Deedee sat down uninvited. A moment later there was a slight movement and the blonde leaped up with a sharp painful cry and a spurt of unladylike words, and Lanahan thought for a moment there was going to be a catfight right there, but in the end the blonde went away in search of other prey, and somehow Beans did not seem quite so uncomfortable with Deedee.

Lanahan took another drink. *Lord*, he thought in amused amazement, *I can't be getting that old...*

But he felt old—or perhaps not old—eased; which might be the same thing with another name. And now he didn't want to get drunk either, and he picked up his bottle and turned it over to the bar man who measured it by eye and set the price which Lanahan paid. When he looked over toward the table, Beans and Deedee were gone, and he shrugged and walked over to the card table where Tennessee played, watched idly a moment, and then not so idly.

CHAPTER SIXTEEN

Something was working in Tennessee. Lanahan knew the signs, for he had been working, riding, eating, sleeping in his near company long months now; the thing might not show to an outsider, but Tennessee was too carefully careless. His chair was pushed a trifle back, his slow drawling voice slower and softer; his hands, rough with work, a trifle grimed at the knuckles despite his last scrubbing before coming on the town, showed just the slightest tension in the way the fingers touched his cards, then utterly relaxed. The cards came around, and

Tennessee went half across the table in a catlike lunge; his strong narrow hand trapped deck and hand together for the dealer; his softly snarling voice said, 'That's twice, now, and too many; you're tryin' to use me for youh fool, misteh!'

He twisted his hand and the dealer's hand turned with it, palm up with the bottom of the deck showing an ace; Tennessee said softly, savagely, 'You're not even a good tinhorn, misteh.'

His man, who had not said a word, showed a narrow bitter smile, and then his eyes dropped from Tennessee's face. He pulled his hand free and let the cards spill and took a careful slanting look around the table, he pulled back and slid his chair away; almost magically a little drawer opened before him, and his hand fell there, came up, all in one smooth motion which had no beginning other than his initial prosaic movement back. Tennessee drew and fired all in one motion, a short snatching movement that exploded at the end in a shocking club of sound.

The sledgehammer blow threw the man back in his chair; his weight and momentum snapped some brittle slat, and he slammed on back, scarcely hampered by that small initial resistance; he arched back and tumbled, in a series of dreadful soft thudding sounds half hidden by the splintering of the chair.

Tennessee took one short step back so that his revolver covered the rest of them at the table; the billow of white smoke spewing in a thick club form spread wider; Lanahan remembered the house man on the stairway landing at the rear of the place and without conscious thought he wheeled and drew and slanted the .44 up at that man just as he dropped the legs of his tipped chair and reached for the short-sawed shotgun against the railing.

'Come on down out of there,' said Lanahan. 'Leave that gun where it is.' That call stopped the last of the movement in the room; men had leaped or ducked or simply frozen at the ear-smiting roar of Tennessee's shot.

'Boss man,' said Tennessee's curiously thick but still soft voice, 'don't put yourself out none. I got this head heah by the tail, an' I'll swing it.'

'Outside,' said Lanahan. 'Cover my back. I'm comin' out.'

'My fight, boss man. I ain't runnin' from nothin'.'

'Outside,' said Lanahan tonelessly, keeping a careful sweep of his eyes on his end of the room, watching the house man come reluctantly down the short stair flight, hands held well out and resenting it, the rest of them simply watchful. 'Get out of here, and we'll settle our part of it outside.'

He stood a long tingling moment longer, then knew from soft sounds behind him that Tennessee was moving. He started moving backward after that sound, keeping a close attention on that house man who was undoubtedly still armed in some hidden way and was therefore the most dangerous man in the place; he stepped back and back, finally heard Tennessee's harsh murmur, 'All right, boss man, I've got it from the door.'

He stepped out through the doorway then, instantly hooked Tennessee's elbow with a rough hand, turned him, hustled him on with that hand clamped to his elbow, using his advantage of weight to keep him moving.

'God damn it,' he said bitterly, 'you got to have a man for breakfast every town we hit, Tennessee? How the hell did we get through Boise without you shooting somebody down?'

Tennessee made a sudden strangled sound and tore himself violently free. He made a full turn and raised his pistol, head-high, cried in a strangled sobbing voice, 'Oh, damn you, man! God damn you to hell—leave me alone!'

Lanahan involuntarily flinched back from the threat of the clubbed weapon, bitterly aroused, confused, and a voice cut at them with an authority as sharp as a whipcrack, 'Drop those pistols, the pair of you. Right now!' Lanahan turned on the voice, saw a man short and heavy, with a determined bulldog face, a metal star glinting on his breast, holding low on them with a short double-barreled gun, the two great gaping muzzles black as hell's own pit.

'Drop 'em,' said the man implacably, 'I ain't giving you no chance and no count. You shuck them pistols right now!'

There was no choice at all, save the slim hope of shooting first, and the certain knowledge of what a sawed-off would do at this range discouraged that.

Lanahan moved slowly that there might be no mistaking his intention, let the hammer down to half cock, knowing how touchy and unreliable that was, and slowly and carefully holstered the .44, not wanting to drop it; unbuckled his belt, holding onto one end, felt the heavy holster touch the wooden walk, and let go entirely.

'You got sense,' said the man woodenly. 'Take his. I doubt he has.'

Tennessee's face was a taut watchful wolf's face. He had not moved, he was still undecided, but he had not lowered the revolver in his hand or turned it aside. Lanahan reached up and took hold of it, felt the momentary resistance in Tennessee, the slow relaxation; he took the pistol and stepped back, stooped and laid it atop his own outfit.

'You got something else under that vest?' said the bulldog faced man.

'Ain't nothin' else,' said Tennessee in a bitter voice.

'Come on then,' said the man. 'Let's have your story.'

'I caught him bottom-dealin,' said Tennessee tonelessly, 'I called him, he grabbed a gun, I shot him. There's your story.'

'You're some fast with a gun,' said the man.

'Some,' said Tennessee. He did not look at the man, he did not look at anyone. He stood with his strong narrow hands slightly hooked, his arms a trifle bent, his unreadable look over them, past them, ignoring them while he apparently concentrated on something beyond.

The bulldog faced man said, 'Ira,' and a man stepped up from the crowd. He was handed the shotgun and the quick brutal instruction, 'Hold 'em. If they move, shoot 'em. But I want 'em here when I get back.' He turned away then, shouldered through a ring of spectators which seemingly had risen from the earth, and was gone.

He came back, with a man Lanahan remembered from the card table. 'This the man?'

The witness nodded.

'And McQuillan went for his gun first?'

'He did, but he never made it. Like he was struck by lightnin', b' God.'

'Wonder he wasn't struck 'fore this.' Then, to Lanahan, 'Who're you?'

'Clay Lanahan. I'm roddin' that AP Connected herd out on the hill. This man works for me. He didn't have much choice. That tinhorn was set to beef him. He just didn't make it, is all, or you'd have somebody else under your gun. What did you expect him to do—stand there and get shot?'

'No. But he could have pulled out of the game anytime.'

Tennessee said in a soft passionless voice, 'What are you chewin' it oveh, foah? I killed the sonofabitch. I'd do it again. You don't need to chew it no fineh than that.'

'You might be glad we chew it a little. Twenty years ago the Regulators would have had you swingin' from a rafter by now, just on general principles, probably. So don't push it. I know you boys come off the trail sometimes figgerin' to tree yourself a town; not this town, mister, not while I'm in it. All right, it looks plain enough. But I want you out of town. You—Lanahan, you said your name was?—you take care of him; take his pistol and don't give it back till you're out of town. I don't want you back.'

'All right,' said Lanahan. 'But I'll have to come back. I've got to round up my crew and supplies.'

'Leave your guns in camp then; you've used up all the trouble you've got coming.'

'All right,' said Lanahan steadily, 'if you'll guarantee me some friend of his won't take me on after you've pulled my teeth. This town ain't that tame.'

The bulldog faced man showed a small sardonic smile. 'McQuillan didn't have a friend. Get what you need and clear out. Keep him out of town. All right, go along.' With that, he took his short shotgun and bucked a path through the spectators, calling out in a short cranky tone, 'Move along there; nothing to herd up for.'

Silently Lanahan stooped, came up with Tennessee's pistol and his own. He looked up and Tennessee's hand reached out silently, waiting. Lanahan tried to read his expression, could not, and finally handed the weapon to Tennessee, who carefully holstered it, stood motionless, waiting, while Lanahan swung his own belt around his hips and buckled it.

Tennessee said finally, tonelessly, 'You're goin' to pay me off now, boss man?'

'No,' said Lanahan, 'and you're not going to quit. I hired you all the way, and that's the way it is—all the way. Now you'd better get on out to the herd. Anything you need, say so, and I'll get it and bring it out.'

'Don't do me no favors,' said Tennessee.

He wheeled away, went down the street perhaps fifty feet, ducked under the tie rail and took the tie knot out of his *mecate* with a single snap, tucked the coiled line under his belt as he stepped up into the saddle, backed and sidled his mount free and rode out without a backward look. Lanahan sighed, a long lingering sound, and went to find his own mount at the livery corral.

* * *

He found Tennessee crouched broodingly over the dying coals of the campfire by the chuck wagon. He lifted his head to the sound of Lanahan's coming, then stared back into the fire. Lanahan got down, made a cigarette, thrust a small stick into the coals until it caught a ball of flame at its end, and lighted up.

'I shouldn't have called you like that in town,' he said. 'I had no right to do that.'

'Sho,' said Tennessee. His eyes were as yellow as a cat's eyes in the dull glow of the coals. With slow, careful motions, Tennessee reached behind him, brought a couple of dry sticks around and fed them to the coals; their burning light spread and grew, pushing back the dark. 'I wish I could get drunk,' he said musingly. 'I had a full pint in my warbag, and I drunk it all since I left town, and I can't get drunk. You got any whisky on you,

Clay?'

'No,' said Lanahan. Then, remembering, he got up and rooted through the chuck wagon and finally turned up a quart bottle, unlabeled, half full. 'Best I can do,' he said, coming back to the fire.

Tennessee took it, held it so that the firelight shone through it, twisted out the cork and tipped it up, his throat making a series of racking stretches as he swallowed, showing no more sign of its strength than if it had been water.

He lowered the bottle, sat staring at nothing, blankly, consideringly, finally said, 'No, that's not it,' hammered the cork home with the heel of his hand, and set the bottle aside. 'It don't do no good,' he said.

He looked into the fire. 'I neveh went to be a killer,' he said. 'You think theah's somethin' born in a man to keep him in trouble?'

'Wouldn't know,' said Lanahan.

'I was raised rough,' said Tennessee in a musing voice. 'My folks was hill people. My daddy was a straight man. He had his ways, but he was a straight-out man. He got killed—shot in the back. I laid for the man that did it—I laid for him for nineteen days. I neveh shot him in the back, either. I stepped out and whistled, an' he seen me, an' knew who it was, an' I shot him. He had his gun, but I shot him, an' left him right theah an' I never went back, because theah wasn't any of my family left but some aunts an' cousins, but I neveh figgered myself a killer. He shot my daddy in the back.' He lifted his eyes from the fire, stared into the dark, brought his attention back to the fire. 'I was fourteen years old,' he said.

He raked a limb through the coals, stirring them, staring into them as if he sought the answer to something within their terrible glow.

'Neveh went to kill anybody, no time. I killed two Indians, 'paches, down in the Arizona country. They jumped me, on a lone night camp. I killed a man in Baker City; I killed a man tonight; God damn it, Clay, why'd it have to be like that—I neveh went to be a killer!' His yellow eyes swung intently on Lanahan; on his face was a look of taut waiting; his voice was a cry of desperation. He had said the whisky hadn't touched him, but it showed in his eyes and around his mouth. He was a man made miserable by what he had done, and he was loosened in his self-control.

Lanahan said more harshly than he intended, not meaning to set himself in judgment, 'You could throw that pistol away; bury it some place. If it wasn't there when your temper let go, maybe it would help.'

Tennessee stared at him, his yellow eyes

alight with something, his voice little more than a harsh whisper. 'Sho. An' you'd have been in an alley in Baker with youh money belt gone an' youh belly showin' if I hadn't had the gun that time; I'd of been dead, when I walked in on it. I'd of been dead tonight—he neveh looked at my gun; I'd of been dead, or he'd of made me crawl under his gun . . . Don't you preach at me like that; you throwed down on that man up on the balcony; you held 'em while we come out of theah. It's no answer—you know it!'

'Suppose not,' said Lanahan. 'Have your drink.'

'That's no answer either,' said Tennessee.

He reared up suddenly, stood tall and lean in the wash of light; he held out his hands as if to warm them at the fire, but he was studying them as they trembled, became still, trembled again; some fleeting thought made him change expression, and then he turned quickly, walked out into the dark, got his bedroll, and came back with it just to the outer fringe of light. He grunted his way out of his boots, unshipped his belt and holster, tucked them into the canvas cover, crawled into the bedroll still wearing his hat, tipped down to shield his face.

Lanahan waited until he was sure there was no more to be said, and then mounted and rode out to check his herd.

* * *

He went back into town in the early morning, in a Sunday quiet, a pale and pearly light all around him in this hushed time before sunup; as he turned in on the main street a shaft of the first sunlight touched the dust like a benediction. He went to the hotel, glanced into the dining room and saw a few early risers waiting breakfast; he went on to Eileen's room and tapped on the door.

Apparently she was up already, for it was little more than a moment before she opened the door for him.

She looked fresh and rested and she had a smile for him, and he decided that bad news could wait until they had eaten.

'You're an early riser, for Sunday,' she said.

Trying to fall into her cheerful mood, he said, 'I just got hungry. Sleep well?—I mean it didn't get too noisy, did it?'

'I slept wonderfully. And you?'

He had the feeling she was asking more than the simple question, and he slid a devilish sidelong look at her and grinned without answering, and saw a little searching look come on her.

Breakfast was better than supper had been. Eggs, fresh eggs, bacon—not salt side pork—flapjacks and honey. Eileen sighed.

'Eggs. How long has it been since I've had an egg for breakfast? And real butter! Clay, why is it that we've got some fifteen hundred cows with us day and night, and not a smidgen of butter?'

He laughed. 'I'll hold one, if you'll milk her,' he promised. 'I don't think anybody else in the outfit ever milked a cow in their lives. Beans, maybe.' The thought of Beans brought a smile to his face, and Eileen said, 'What are you grinning at now?'

He said easily, 'The thought of you milking one of those proddy old range cows.'

'I'll bet I could do it,' she said challengingly.

He looked at her a little more soberly. 'Maybe you could,' he said, 'you go pretty lively when your dander's up.'

She said, 'You must think I'm an awfully strongwilled creature. What an expression to use.'

He said thoughtfully, 'I didn't mean it quite that way. A weak woman wouldn't have made it this far. She wouldn't look like you do this morning.'

She looked at him steadily. 'Thank you,' she said.

He felt a trifle flushed, and said, 'You going to eat those eggs, or do I get to clean 'em up?'

'You'll think I'm lively if you try to steal these eggs. Will we be here any longer than today?'

He caught that. In Baker City it would likely have been a demand, or possibly a statement of how long it would be. But with that encouraging thought came the knowledge that he had to tell her.

'I'd thought to lay over,' he said, 'but if your little gripsack is all packed, we should go right on this morning. Ebe has the chuck wagon loaded and ready, and we should be going on.'

She studied his face, he thought, but finally said merely, 'My, you are in a hurry, aren't you?'

'I'll go find the crew,' he said. He paid the waiter and went out into the street.

He turned a corner and saw Beans coming down an outside stairway. He looked sleepy and scrubbed clean, and in his eyes was the look of a man who sees distant and pleasant things. He moved slowly, and when Lanahan spoke to him, he flushed violently red, and then that look came back, and he nodded almost indifferently when Lanahan told him to find his horse and get on back to the herd.

Lanahan watched him go, smiling wryly; Beans wasn't anybody's kid any more. He'd ridden the river with the men—damn good men—and held up his end. He'd earned his pay and he'd been to town, and he'd seen the elephant, and he wasn't a kid any more, and he never would be again.

Lanahan got Eileen Prather's horse and led it to the hotel. He knew when he saw her that she had heard something; it showed on her face, but she did not ask him just then. He buckled the portmanteau behind the cantle for her, made a stirrup of his hands and helped her mount; then he swung up and rode beside her.

As they left the town, she said, 'Clay, what happened? I heard a man talking; when he saw me he stopped—but something is wrong.'

He said bluntly, not looking at her, 'Tennessee killed a man.' He heard her quick gasp, and the following words, 'What did they do to him? Where is he?'

'He's at the camp. I don't think anybody will do anything. But we're not wanted here; we'll have to push on.'

She was silent a while, and then she sounded somehow hesitant, almost fearful. 'Was it . . . did he . . .?'

'It wasn't—murder, if that's what you're thinking. You can say it's never right to kill a man; and yet you put any man where he must kill or be killed, and generally he'll make his try. It was a rough game, and Tennessee had that choice. He killed his man. That's all.'

'Ah,' she said softly, and he could not tell what she meant by that sound. Then: 'What caused it?'

'A card game. It could have been anything; a horse, a woman, a shove on the street; those things happen; it's a rough country and no way around it.'

'But must it be? Isn't it rough men who make a rough country?'

'Now that could be. Either way, there it is. What do you do with it but meet it and match it? It's a hard thing to explain, but there it is.'

'And a woman couldn't be expected to understand it.'

'I didn't say that.' He looked at her, but her eyes were straight ahead.

'No,' she said coolly, 'you didn't.' They rode on in silence to the stirring camp.

* * *

The herd went on. Bozeman. The Yellowstone—an easy crossing on a long sandy riffle. Low water. Bighorn Mountains looming ahead. *Git along there, you aggervatin' brute. Git on up ahead and see your new home. Yi-yi-yi-YI! git along!*

* * *

The basin. A mighty land. A man could stand in his stirrups and see a hundred miles. It wasn't a basin, it was a world, with distant purple smudges to mark its edges. They'd called it the Great American Desert, some of the early far-roamers, and it was true, there was little kindness or gentleness in this mighty land. Here was the stuff of empires, for big men, strong men, but it would not come to them from wishfulness. It would be earned; it would be paid for. A mighty land. Here they came to the end of their journey.

CHAPTER SEVENTEEN

The actual delivery of the herd was anticlimax. You brought a herd into Abilene or Dodge, ran a tally, turned them over to the buyers or shunted them into the pens, and the job came to a quick and definite end. Then there was the town, end of the trail, booming and roaring and whooping it up to entertain you, and you hitched up your pants and rolled your spurs and took 'er in, ready to fight, fiddle or frolic, with the timid riding the drag.

Here, it was the inertia of nigh a thousand miles drifting to a halt, running down like a tired old clock that couldn't decide whether to strike thirteen or just quit. A multitude of pestering detail with no dividing line to mark the end. Lanahan ran his final tally.

Two thousand six head had been put on the trail at Baker City. Four lost on the

Snake, one on the Weiser. Twenty-four in the blistering hell of the lava beds. But the calf wagon had done its work well. The final tally stood one thousand nine hundred seventy-seven cows and steers. Two hundred fifty-one calves. Four unbranded steers that had joined the herd at various points along the drive. Grand total: Two thousand two hundred thirty-two.

Lanahan had the crew split the herd into bunches, move them out like spokes in a wheel to populate the range. They were in good season. The cattle would have time to orient themselves, find where water and shelter were best before winter hit. He rode down to the house.

Eileen came out onto the long porch that ran along one whole side of the house. She had her sleeves rolled up and her head bound in a turban made of flour sacking. A four-cornered piece of the same material was an apron, one corner pinned at her bosom and two tied together about her narrow waist. She leaned a broom against the door frame as she came out.

'Didn't mean to disturb you,' said Lanahan.

She gave him a rueful smile. 'You did me a favor. A house that's left empty for a year is heartbreaking. I was hoping something would give me an excuse to stop a few minutes.' She looked up at him questioningly, and he swung down, dropped his reins, and stepped up onto the porch. He fished in his shirt pocket, found his notebook, and ripped out a page and handed it to her.

'Full tally,' he said. 'That winds up the herd. I'll have a couple of the crew get at fixing up the corrals tomorrow, and Eben should be back with your supplies in a day or so.' He looked at her, and then away, dug up his tobacco and papers to give his fingers something to do.

'You'll need a couple of hands,' he said. 'I'd recommend George Bristow and Tex Walker. Both good steady men, good hands.'

Eileen said demurely, but with a little teasing note in her voice, 'Not Tennessee?'

Lanahan retorted shortly, 'Not Tennessee. He'd probably stay if you asked him, but you'd have to fire him or marry him within two months.'

'Is that so bad?' He couldn't make out her tone, but he felt a little warmth coming to his cheeks.

'Good for him, maybe. Bad for you. He's a fiddlefoot. He'd break your heart and leave you barefoot in a year.' Then he had the grace to give her a little grin.

'Besides,' he added, 'he drew his pay. He's been here a week, and that's too long in one place for him.' He dropped his cigarette, carefully rubbed it out with his toe, and said, without looking up from this absorbing task, 'You really ought to have someone to stay with you, anyway. Another woman. It won't be so good here alone.'

'There'll be two men here,' she said with a little asperity.

'That's what I mean,' he said. He stepped off the porch and mounted again. From the safe height of the saddle he said, 'I'm sending Jed on with our horses to my claim tomorrow. I imagine I'll be finished up here in another day.' He remembered something then, and fumbled inside his shirt and rode closer to hand the money belt down to her. 'There's a little left to tide you over for a bit.'

She said uncertainly, 'But that's your money, and even so, it doesn't begin to pay you. I can't take it.'

'You're broke,' he said bluntly, 'and you've got obligations to meet. I sold some of my horses down at the trader's; got my price and I'm satisfied; I can see daylight ahead. I wouldn't be satisfied gougin' you for what I got coming. You get squared away, and then you can think about my payoff. It's late for selling, but some of the others out in the basin might take some of those steers at a decent price, if you need more ready money. If you can hang on till spring without too bad a winter kill, you ought to be seeing your own daylight.'

She said steadily, looking up at him, 'I

can't thank you. You've done too much for any thanks of mine. I hope you understand that.'

He grinned faintly. 'Why,' he said, '"we're neighbors.'

She said, 'That's sort of funny, isn't it? I never knew of you before Grande Ronde, and then came all this way to find your claim is practically next door.'

'If you can call ten miles next door,' he said, 'and I guess it is, out here. Well, you've got the makings of a fair spread here. For my money this foothill country is the best range any way you look at it. Sheltered better in winter, pretty sure of water in the summer; a latecomer can't get at any of the big steady rivers any more; all sewed up. It's a good layout.'

It was. It would be better, after her union with Homer Flagg, for his big spread was anchored on one of the valuable river stretches, and would spread across a vast open range to link up here with several pretty dependable feeder creeks crosswoven in the second of the cattleman's two essentials; water and grass. He thought of that but did not say it, for he felt a taste of bitterness in it.

'I'll be getting on,' he said. 'You be sure to have Eben put that chuck wagon under shelter. You'll be wanting to use it again one day. The crew's paid up through this week. You'll need some tinkerin' and carpenterin' around here; they might not like it, but they'll do it if you point 'em right. I guess that's about all.'

She smiled at him. 'Still the conscientious one, aren't you? I appreciate it, Clay. And don't be a stranger around here. We've come too far for that.'

He said, 'Sure,' but he thought of Homer Flagg, and knew there would be nothing here for him; he touched his hat and put his horse in motion.

He had his own work, at his claim, and Jed's. He went at it with such ferocious zeal that Jed, toward the end of the sixth consecutive daylight-to-dark driving, growled, 'Pardner, I got just two arms and two laigs. Did I hire out for a horse, I'm entitled to a new harness, dammit.'

Lanahan growled back, 'Might as well give up to it, boy, you're draft stock; if you were worth a damn for breedin' I'd have you in your own private pen. Now you goin' to snake those timbers down here, or do we wait for fall flood to wash 'em down?'

* * *

Homer Flagg rode a tired horse into the dooryard at Eileen Prather's house, pulled up, but did not dismount. Eileen came through the doorway and said, 'Homer! Where did you come from?'

‘From the trader’s,’ he said. ‘From my place before that. I had to find out from an outsider that you’d got here finally. Do I rate an invitation to get down?’

Her smile faded under his straightforward tone, and she eyed him searchingly and then said coolly, ‘I don’t remember you ever having to have a special invitation before, Homer. Of course, get down, come in.’

He said, ‘Thank you. Maybe before I didn’t have to wonder where I stood with you.’ He swung down, the saddle squealing under his shifting weight. He walked to the porch. ‘You’re looking good, Eileen.’

‘Thank you,’ she said. ‘Come in. I’ve some coffee. Are you hungry?’

‘Ah, Eileen,’ he said. ‘You know I’m hungry.’ His arms reached out and caught her and brought her to him. He kissed her, not hard, but not tentatively either, and then as suddenly released that pressure and said, ‘Don’t you feel any more than that for me?’

‘Of course,’ she said. She waited, then broke that hesitation by drawing back, moving him with her. ‘Come in,’ she said. ‘Leave the door open, will you? It still seems dusty—unaired, here. It’s a pretty day. I love this weather. And how do you like my house?’

‘It’s a house,’ he said bluntly, not looking around at the room they entered. ‘The only house I give a damn about is my house with you in it. When is that going to be, Eileen? When are we going to stop this pussyfooting around?'

She said, 'You're edgy, Homer. I'm still a little tired. There is so much to be done. Do we have to decide right now?'

'Yes, by God, we do,' he said.

'Sit down, Homer,' she said. 'I'll bring some coffee.'

She went into the kitchen and Homer sent a quick scanning survey around the room, dropped his hat on the table near by, seated himself. Eileen brought cups and coffee. Homer did not taste his.

He said, 'You're putting me off. What is it, another man?'

'No,' she said. 'You know it isn't, Homer. I told you. I am still a little tired. There is so much to do...'

He kept his eyes closely, broodingly on her. He stirred himself a little in his chair. He said heavily, 'You're putting things in the way, and there's no need of it. You're my woman, Eileen. I knew it from the moment I saw you; back when your father came through to find this place. He didn't find this place, I brought him to it. He didn't find his Grande Ronde cattle, I found them for him. Looking back, sometimes I think he was putting things in the way too. I didn't care, as long as it brought me near enough to you.'

'That's—very—flattering, Homer.' She

turned her cup by its handle, gently, watching the almost invisible movement of the dark liquid within.

'It wasn't meant to be. It's meant to be a statement of fact. I could have a dozen women, as easy as that.' He snapped his strong fingers. 'I don't want any other women. It was that coolness of yours, I think, that way you could look at a man, at anybody at all, and be yourself, without using any woman's tricks to ram it down a man's throat that you are a woman. I'm a big man; I'm going to be bigger. Where I go I want a woman who can stand with me, grow with me; I don't want some soft featherbrained female dragging me back hanging around my neck. You're cool, and you're strong, and there's a fire under all that, and I want that too. That's all I want. I don't want any of these other things you own. If every acre of this land was burned over, if this house was dynamited to splinters, if every damned head that carried your brand went over a cliff into the river, I wouldn't even turn my head to watch it happen. I could pay for every dime of it by scratching my name on a piece of paper, and it wouldn't mean any more than that to me. You can put me off—you can bring things between us—I'll still be right here waiting. Now when is it going to be?'

His rising voice had brought her attention

closely on him. She watched him and then looked down again.

'I don't know,' she said. there was uncertainty in her voice, and he caught that, staring at her with his unwavering regard.

He said softly, 'That's it, then. You don't know. You don't know what you want. I hadn't thought to find it in you, but it's all right. You just don't know what it is you want. Come here, Eileen.'

She gave him a look, a brief smile, then looked down at her hands, which had left the cup and were working together, as if smoothing some fine invisible fabric between them. She shook her head slightly. 'I'm not waiting for you to sweep me off my feet,' she said.

'You don't know,' he said. 'It's that way sometimes. You have to be shown what it is you want.' He moved easily off his chair, smiling, reaching a hand to her as an experienced handler might reach out to a nervous animal; his smile, his movements showing the confidence of wisdom and experience as she rose in her turn, moving away before him. He followed, not pressing, firmly, smoothly, gently—implacably. He put his hands on her with that same firm gentleness, brought her close without effort, brought his face down to hers with a slowly increasing pressure.

She rolled her head and broke her lips

free. 'No, Homer,' she said. 'No. That isn't it.'

'You don't know,' he said, gently implacable. 'You've never had the chance to know. So I'll show you. You've held that fire for so long you don't know how to let it go. I'll show you.'

He brought his head down again, and she avoided it. This time she thrust herself away, in real strength, sought earnestly to escape, and found herself unable to touch the strength of his embrace.

'Don't fight me,' he said softly. 'Don't fight it. Come to me, Eileen. Come to me and let it go. Let me show you.'

She threw herself against his encaging arms with all her strength, and could not escape. A kind of frenzy came on her, a need to escape, and she writhed in that entrapment, silently and ferociously, and then almost despairingly, for her strength had no more effect than if she had been hooped round with steel. A ragged note born of passion came into the gentleness of his voice, a husky roughness of certainty. 'Ah,' he said. 'No use fighting it. Sweet Eileen.'

A soft sound came into the room, a soft, polite, coughing sound. Homer's whole body went rigid, a reaching strength came on him that made the other as nothing. He wheeled, turning her with him, in an effortless swing, to face Tennessee, who stood lounging in the open doorway, one shoulder against the jamb, hip-shot, showing the sharply outlined curve of the butt of his holstered revolver in silhouette against the sunlight behind him.

He said softly, 'Interruptin' somethin'?' in a tone of quiet inquiry.

'You sonofabitch,' roared Homer Flagg. 'You sneaking bastard!' His arms fell away and he wheeled further and took one driving charging stride. Tennessee snapped the pistol from its holster in a motion as fast and impossible to follow as that of a striking snake. '*Move easy!*'

Homer caught his momentum with reaction as powerful as his drive; he stopped, but he was poised, and was no less threatening in his stillness.

'Don't jump at me like that,' said Tennessee. 'You reach foah me, misteh, an' you'll be kickin' on that floor with a hole in youh belly big enough to set a fence post.'

'I'm not armed,' said Homer thickly. 'You sneaking dog.'

'I called when I came,' said Tennessee. 'Maybe you wasn't listenin'. What you want I should do with him, Miss Eileen?'

Eileen said through lips suddenly stiff and cold, 'I don't know. I don't care. Just so he goes.' A sleeve had been torn at the shoulder seam of her dress; from her struggle or Homer's hands she did not know. Her hair was down, loose on her shoulders, and she could feel a deep-seated trembling inside her, and tried to keep it from her voice. 'Just get him out of here—please!'

Tennessee took a prowling half-step forward.

'Get out of my way,' said Homer from deep in his throat. Tennessee said softly, 'Go around me ... big man. Walk easy.'

Homer trembled with the effort to hold himself in. His arms were half bent at his sides, his square knuckles were white with pressure. Almost he leaned into the first motion of charging, and the muzzle of the pistol moved upward just the slightest fraction in instant response.

Homer's weight shifted, his foot slid into its first circling step. His hip bumped the table, and he thrust it aside with an effortless movement of his hand. He went around Tennessee, who shifted just enough to keep him under the gun. He stepped through the door. Tennessee sighed almost soundlessly. His eyes flicked at Eileen, around the room, and his tight feral grin showed. 'He fo'got his hat,' he said softly.

He caught it up and stepped outside. He caught the hammer back and eased it down, spun the cylinder with practiced ease and let the hammer nose on the empty shell that carried it safe, holstered the weapon without looking at it.

Homer walked with a stiff striding gait to

his horse. He swung into the saddle. There was a rifle with its sheathed barrel lashed under the stirrup, but he did not touch it. His face showed nothing now save its normal steadfast determination.

He looked down at Tennessee. 'Is this your man, Eileen?' Only the thickness of his voice showed his feelings.

'No,' she said. She stood in the doorway, making no effort to straighten her appearance, watching Homer with steady unforgiving eyes.

'Lanahan then,' he said. 'He'll never get you.'

'You couldn't force me, so it has to be somebody else. Go away, Homer.' Her voice was pure contempt.

Still he held his mount short-reined, and Eileen said clear-voiced, 'Give me your gun, Tennessee.'

'You won't need it, Miss Eileen,' said Tennessee. He scaled Homer's hat, so that Homer caught it with quick reflex motion before it struck him in the face. 'Theah's youh hat, misteh. Move.'

Homer held his intolerant look on them both a moment longer, then hauled his mount about and drove the animal into a hard driving run. Eileen wheeled away from the door, paused, turned back. 'Thank you,' she said to Tennessee.

'Sho,' he said. His alert yellowish eyes

watched her steadily. He said, 'You want to learn neveh to tease a mean dog, Miss Eileen.'

'I wasn't—teasing him, Tennessee.'

'He thought you was. You got a gun?'

'Yes. But he won't be back.'

'Maybe. If he does, ain't nothin' but a bullet goin' to stop him. You mind, now, Miss Eileen.'

She said steadily, 'You take care too, Tennessee.'

He grinned suddenly. 'Some of the trails I've rode, Miss Eileen, I growed an extra pair of eyes on the back of my neck. He ketches me, he's maybe goin' to wish he had some way to let go.'

He turned half away, his face sobering, then turned back. 'Miss Eileen,' he said swiftly, 'I've been a pretty triflin' man. Never had any reason to do any other way. But now maybe somethin's changed, an'...'

Eileen said swiftly, 'Tennessee. Don't. I—think I know what you are going to say. Please don't. I don't want to hurt you. I like you too much to hurt you.'

For just a moment a flickering light seemed to show behind his eyes. Then the stiffness of his face broke into his familiar mocking carelessness, and he grinned and flipped a deprecating hand.

'Why, Miss Eileen,' he said, 'how's a man goin' to know less he asks? Take care, Miss

Eileen.' He wheeled then, walked stiffly and hurriedly around the side of the house, toward the rapping woodpecker sounds the other hands had been making at their repair work.

Eileen watched him go; when he was out of sight, she felt herself let go; the careful restraint she had held went rushing out like water behind a collapsing dam, and she had a rough, unladylike seige of hysterics in her bedroom with the door closed, her face buried in her pillow when it got too bad, almost horrifiedly feeling herself go all to pieces—and at long last, patiently, tiredly, picking them all up, bringing them back together and under her controlled will.

It took quite a while, but before she left the bedroom, she found the light .38 caliber revolver her father had given her, reloaded it, and put it where she could find it quickly. She changed her dress, washed and rewashed her face, re-did her hair. When Eben Longquist came gruffly banging at the back door wanting to know where she wanted the extra supplies from the chuck wagon stored, she felt in command of herself. At least Eben didn't seem to notice anything.

She watched when Eben called the hands to supper at the ramshackle cookhouse elled off the bunkhouse. She did not see Tennessee. She left the window to eat her own solitary meal.

Missy, she told herself grimly, *nobody said it would be easy...*

CHAPTER EIGHTEEN

There was more provision on Lanahan's claim for horses than for men. The corrals of peeled poles and immense, deepset posts were sprawled up the draw behind the cabin, each corral staggered in relation to the others so that removal of a few poles allowed animals to be herded from one into another. They bordered the creek so that water was available to any animal in any corral.

The cabin was compact, butted up against a rock face against which the chimney clung, the other three sides of peeled logs, with a split board door hung on leather hinges. A shed roof supported by poles jutted to one side. The roof was shakes, and the furniture a bare minimum. Two bunks, a plank table, stove, shelves. A wooden box nailed to the wall for a dish cupboard, two barrels for storage bins, a water keg. The clothes closets were pegs driven into the wall, on any one of which was likely to be hung a spare shirt, a hackamore that needed mending, sundry bits of leather to be cut into lacing, a worn horseshoe with a bit of usefulness still left in it.

Eileen Prather rode up the wide shallow draw that was almost a small valley, took off her hat and shook out her hair as the cooler breeze swept down to lift the late autumn heat from her. She sent a warning call to the cabin as she rode up, but got no reply. She rode up almost to the door, called again, then crossed over to the side where a jutting boulder made a fair mounting block, carefully disengaged herself from the sidesaddle and managed to dismount alone. She peered in at the cabin's clutter, made a face, turned to look down across the corrals, but still saw nothing but the few penned horses.

For a moment, she strolled aimlessly about the packed dirt dooryard, then looked in the doorway again, and with a little shrug, started to unbutton her jacket.

A man alone certainly makes a mess of things, she thought.

* * *

Jed and Lanahan cut out the half-dozen horses they wanted, and let the rest of them go, herding the half-dozen at a brisk trot for a couple of miles to work some of the ginger out of them and take their minds off the herd they'd just left. Where a little stream ran through a lush swale, they eased up and let the animals drink, rode upstream and bellied down to quench their own thirst.

Afterward they lay back, lolled on the grass and rolled smokes, willing to take a break after being out since daylight after this bunch.

Jed fired up and said through a cloud of blue smoke, 'That Beans kid hit me for a chance to come up with us again. Saw him down at the trader's.'

Lanahan said briefly, 'We're not big enough for another man yet. He's riding for Mill Iron anyway, isn't he?'

'Chore-boyin' half the time. Says he never signed up to be no flunky. You give him big ideas, makin' him a full hand on the drive.'

'Too bad,' said Lanahan. He stretched out flat on the grass and blew a plume of smoke straight up, regarded the cigarette with distaste, and threw it away, not half smoked. He locked his hands behind his head and looked up into the blue distance of the sky.

Jed looked at him sidelong, smiled crookedly and said, 'Your system's full of poison. Go on down to the trader's and get a load on and pick a fight and sweat some of it out of you.'

Lanahan grunted, closed his eyes, and said, 'A drink isn't worth a fifty-mile ride.'

'Seen you ride farther for one.'

Lanahan snorted and rolled over onto his belly without opening his eyes and cradled his head on his crossed arms. Jed Martindale drew on his cigarette and went on musingly, 'They're talkin' maverick down at the trader's. Some's talkin' vigilante.'

Lanahan's voice, muffled against his sleeve, said, 'Nothing against mavericking. A critter without a brand belongs to the man who brands him.'

'Yeah, but they say somebody's gettin' nearsighted. Runs his mark over the old one so good you got to skin the hide to spot it.'

'Who says?'

'Well, it's a funny thing. Homer Flagg's name keeps coming up.'

'So,' said Lanahan, 'he'll hang somebody and it'll quiet down.'

'So they figger,' said Jed placidly. 'Only they're still talkin' behind their hands. Mebbe I heard somethin' I shouldn't, but somebody mentioned Tennessee.'

Lanahan's shoulders gave a little twitch, and then his voice came, muffled as before. 'That's his lookout,' he said indifferently.

'Some say he makes too big a track to suit Flagg,' Jed pursued.

'Still his lookout,' said Lanahan.

'You're a cheerful bastard today,' observed Jed.

'Yes, and you nag like an old woman.'

Jed said, apropos of nothing. 'Funny them two ain't got hitched yet. I'm beginnin' to wonder if they will. Maybe you're missin' a good thing there, pardner.'

Lanahan said jeeringly, not pretending to misunderstand. 'Hell, yes. I got a lot to toss in that game, ain't I? Half-interest in a shoestring horse outfit. Hell, either of 'em could buy us out and throw us out with the empty cans and never miss it. She'll marry Flagg; they're too much alike, not to.'

'That's a dirty thing to say. He ain't fit to marry up with a bitch wolf. She's some strong-headed, but she ain't like him.'

'Whyn't you sashay down there an' put your bid, then?'

'Like I say,' said Jed, 'you're a cheerful bastard today.'

Lanahan rolled over and got up. 'Let's get these knotheads down to the corrals,' he said.

* * *

Eileen started guiltily at the sound of the horse outside, put the broom aside, and hastily pulled the sleeves of her white blouse down. With a touch of flurried irritation she realized a fine mist of dust still hung in the air, and that she was warm and flushed from her work. It was bad enough to be cleaning a man's cabin uninvited, without being caught at it.

The horse came slowly across the packed earth outside, stopped; she could hear the unusual heaviness of its breathing. Even as she walked to the door she noticed that the rider was slow to dismount, and it was only as she took the last step that she heard the creaking of the saddle and the thud of his feet hitting the ground. She stepped through the door and found herself smiling directly into the eyes of Tennessee.

Something flickered in his pale, yellowed eyes, and she felt the smile freezing on her face. She hadn't seen him in a month; since he'd come to call last, and the episode with Homer. Now his expression was stiff, almost shocked, and then suddenly his mouth curved in its tight sardonic grin, and he said softly, 'Playin' house?'

She saw the way he carried his arm then, realized that he had his hand inside his unbuttoned shirt to support the wrist, and that his twisted neckerchief was a clumsy bandage for his forearm.

'What's the matter, Tennessee?' She tried to keep her voice unexcited, but did not quite succeed.

'Little trouble,' he said easily, but two lines were cut deep into his brown leather face from nostril to mouth corner. He walked toward her, looked over her shoulder, and his hawk eyes swept the cabin in one long look. 'Where's Lanahan?'

'Why, I don't ...' Then she heard the sound, across the corrals, and saw Lanahan and Jed Martindale hazing a half-dozen horses into the end pen, and said, 'There they are now.'

Tennessee took a long swift step through the doorway, and there sheltered, he gave the corrals a searching inspection.

'So they are,' he murmured. He wheeled away, scouring the shack with his eyes, stepped back to one of the bunks and reached up to a Winchester, hanging in its sheath against the wall. He drew the carbine half out of its sheath, saw Eileen's eyes steadily wondering upon him, shrugged and slid it back. Some inner excitement painted two spots of color on his high-boned cheeks, and his eyes were very bright and intent as he sauntered back to the doorway.

Lanahan rode into the dooryard and swung down out of the saddle, looking at Eileen with a little surprise. 'Hello. This is a surprise.' Then he caught sight of Tennessee just inside the doorway, and said dryly, 'Well.'

'Hope I'm not intrudin',' said Tennessee easily. He gave Lanahan his twisted smile, and said, 'Boss man, I need a horse. Mine's tuckered out.'

Lanahan frowned intently, looking carefully at Tennessee, and then Tennessee stepped out of the door and showed his bandaged arm. 'You're running,' said Lanahan bluntly.

'You could say that,' retorted Tennessee dryly. He had his eyes narrowly on Lanahan's face, intent, watchful.

As they stood facing one another, Eileen was startled by their strange resemblance. Tennessee was lighter, smaller, thinner, whiplike, fair where Lanahan was dark; but with the same high-bridged nose, the bony cheeks, narrow proud jaw; and yet they were not alike at all.

Then Tennessee said, 'Clay, I'm not goin' to beg. I could put a gun on you an' taken what I wanted.'

'Yes,' said Lanahan tonelessly. He stood by his horse, still with one rein in his hand.

'A man shouldn't talk about past favors, either,' said Tennessee, 'an' I wouldn't, except I got no choice. They're comin', Clay, an' they got the rope knotted an' the limb picked. I got to have a horse an' some ca'tridges, an' so I'm goin' to remind you about an alley in Baker City. I got to have 'em, Clay.'

'And if I don't?' Lanahan's face showed nothing.

Tennessee shrugged, and for a second his tight mirthless grin flashed. 'Then it's four steps back to that Winchester on the wall. I'll take a chance on a bullet before I'll stand still for the rope.' Only his taut lips showed the emotion in the man, that and the cords that stood out on the back of his clawed right hand.

Lanahan said abruptly, almost roughly, 'Miss Prather, you'd better take a walk. You won't be asked to tell what you don't know.'

Eileen said a little uncertainly, 'It's a little late for that, isn't it?' She hugged her arms across her breast, wondering a little foolishly if she ought to go inside the cabin for her jacket. Lanahan gave her one of his rare smiles and said in an easier tone, 'I guess you're right.'

He had made up his mind apparently, for he turned half around and called to Jed Martindale, 'Bring that Buster horse up, will you, Jed?' Then he wheeled back on Tennessee.

'I'll give you a horse,' he said, 'and one load of shells. I want your word that you'll clear out. I won't have you shooting on my hands. You're clear for the moment, and I want you to stay clear. Understand?'

Tennessee cried hotly, 'Dammit, a man's got to fight if he's crowded. Don't throw me back to them with my hands empty!'

Lanahan said almost gently, 'That's why I'm giving you just five shells. You won't be tempted to fight it out. You'll keep moving, and maybe you'll get a little of it knocked out of you.' For the first time his voice roughened with his inner feelings. 'Don't think I'm sticking my neck in a rope to take this off your back. I'm giving you one last chance to straighten yourself out—and if you won't have it that way it's better if I give you to them, and help pull the rope myself.'

Tennessee's narrow face went deadly pale, the little fever blotches standing on his bony cheeks like paint marks.

'I'm not a beggah, Lanahan,' he cried in a high singing tone. 'Don't give me a lecture with youh handout.'

Lanahan retorted bluntly, 'If you had begged, I'd have turned you down. Get what I'm saying, Tennessee. You're a friend, and a good man, but you've pulled out of line. Not your gun, or any friend, can pull you out of all of them, Tennessee. You'll have to make up your own mind.'

Jed Martindale came up with a led horse and stopped, his face showing neither approval, disapproval nor even strong interest. Tennessee looked at Lanahan a moment longer, then dropped his eyes and stepped around him to his own fagged animal.

He made clumsy work of the latigos with his one good hand, and Lanahan gently shouldered him aside and stripped the saddle and blanket off, carried them over to the fresh horse and, while Jed led the animal's head with a short hold on the rope, saddled up. He tightened the flank cinch, moving with the restive animal, slipped the hackamore and bridle on, and said over his shoulder, 'Jed, would you rustle some grub and put it in a sack?'

Jed's eyes flicked from Lanahan to Tennessee, showing a dry speculation for the first time, and Eileen said hurriedly, 'I'll do it.'

She went into the cabin, pulled on her jacket, and hurriedly fumbled with the buttons while she found a flour sack. She put in bacon and coffee and salt, a couple of cans of tomatoes, as an afterthought scooped handfuls of flour into a smaller sack and twisted the top and tucked it in so it wouldn't spill. She came out to hear Lanahan say as he looked at Tennessee's arm, 'That wing going to be all right?' Tennessee said tightly, 'It'll have to be.'

Lanahan took the sack from Eileen, hefted it, asked, 'Matches?' She flushed, said, 'Oh, I forgot,' and Lanahan dug into a pocket, thrust the cluster of matches into Tennessee's breast pocket, and then reached out and got Tennessee's pistol.

He flipped open the loading gate and punched out empty cartridge cases, filled five chambers of the cylinder from his own belt. He gave the cylinder one final click, let the hammer down on the empty chamber, dropped the weapon back in its holster and murmured, 'Good luck.'

Tennessee's taut crooked grin showed for an instant and he said softly, 'It's hard to take help when it's begrudged.'

'It's not begrudged,' said Lanahan shortly. 'If they weren't behind you, I'd stake you to a belt of shells, and give you my blessing. But I know you. If you had the means, you'd stop and make a fight of it. Now you'll keep moving.'

'Still bossin' the drive, ain't you, Clay?' murmured Tennessee. 'Maybe you're right.' He very carefully tucked the hackamore *mecate* under his belt in his old familiar gesture, clumsily flipped up the reins and swung into the saddle.

His eyes flicked over to Eileen, and he said mockingly, 'Clay, you betteh marry this woman. She's made out of good stuff.' His hand, holding the reins, reached up and thumped his wide hat brim in a casual salute, and then he rode out, swaying whiplike in the saddle, not hurrying, not looking back.

* * *

Jed Martindale had taken no active part in any of this, but now he moved the run-down animal Tennessee had left to the corrals. Without a word, he leaned down from the saddle to draw three sliding poles back, rode into the corral and hazed out the six or seven head it held, picked up Tennessee's horse with the bunch, and headed them up the draw alongside the creek. He came back, completely phlegmatic and composed, unsaddled his own animal, turned it into the corral, brought the saddle up the little slope and dropped it astraddle a pole rack under the shed roof in a little clash of stiff leather. Seemingly as an afterthought, he pulled out the heavy saddle blanket, dragged it casually by one corner so that it swept the earth behind him, across the yard and down to the creek, where he soused it under and scrubbed at it with a flat rock.

Lanahan stood slackly in the doorway of the shack, one shoulder against the door jamb, thumbs hooked in his belt, staring broodingly down the long wide draw that led out to the open land beyond.

Eileen, with the sense that she had been almost completely forgotten, finally ventured, 'Will—will he be all right?'

Lanahan seemed to know to whom she referred. He said dryly, 'Would a lobo wolf make out? He'll do all right.' Then he looked at her and said in a softer tone, 'I'm sorry you had to be in on it.'

She gave a nervous little laugh. 'Heavens,' she said, 'I never did get to tell you what I came for, did I?' She walked toward him so that he had to stand aside, and went past him into the cabin. The flat leather bag was under her hat on the table, and she picked it up and held it out to him. 'Here,' she said smiling, 'is what I owe you. You have been a good creditor.'

He took it, she thought, reluctantly. She could not read the expression on his face. Then Jed Martindale stepped in through the door and murmured quietly, 'Somebody coming.'

He moved casually over to his bunk, took the Winchester, sheath and all, off the wall, and went back outside. They could hear him whistling softly and working with his saddle just outside.

Lanahan's head lifted alertly, and his eyes came hard on her and then away. 'If you'll ride on up the draw by the corrals and around the hill,' he said, 'you won't be seen.'

Eileen flushed and said tartly, 'I'm not running from anyone.' That brought his eyes sharply back, and she thought he studied her face very casually. Then he shrugged. 'As you say.'

Something kept Eileen where she was as Lanahan stepped out through the doorway. She heard horses coming into the dooryard, and Lanahan's quiet voice greeting them. She heard Homer Flagg's voice answering.

CHAPTER NINETEEN

Somehow, in a calm and fatalistic corner of his mind, Lanahan had known Homer Flagg would come. Tennessee hadn't said—but it had been inevitable. So it was with no surprise at all that he saw Flagg, high above him on his big gelding looking down and demanding, 'Where's Tennessee, Lanahan?'

Lanahan retorted, 'I wouldn't know.'

Homer Flagg said with the stolid bluntness that was his way, 'We trailed him this far. If he hadn't foxed us, we'd have been here sooner. You can't stop us, Lanahan, so you might as well co-operate. Where is he?'

Lanahan said with complete indifference in his voice, 'Kill your own snakes.' He looked at the rest of the men behind Flagg, spotted a couple he knew, but gave them no greeting. Then Flagg said, 'You're not doing yourself any good to buck us. Why don't you be sensible?'

'I don't like to talk to you, Flagg. You rub me the wrong way. Go on about your business.'

Flagg said, 'Jack,' and one of the men pulled out of the group and rode a slow circle clear around the shack, swinging wide toward the corrals. He came back, stopped a little to the side and reported. 'He got a horse here. Somebody drug a blanket over the tracks. There's a horse with a sidesaddle under the shed at the side there.'

Flagg stared down at Lanahan, showing no change in his expression. 'I'll take a look inside your shack, Lanahan,' he said.

'No,' said Lanahan. 'You're here uninvited; you don't step into my house without my permission. Go on about your business.'

Flagg swung down out of his saddle as if he had not heard. Jed Martindale came out from under the shed roof with the Winchester held casually. The one called Jack said, 'I wouldn't,' and held his gun loosely trained on Jed. Lanahan stirred, a rifle muzzle swung on him, a hammer clicked, metallically, dismally.

Homer stood looking at Lanahan a moment, said, 'Keep an eye on him, Jack,' and walked to the cabin, looked inside.

He stood rigid in the doorway, a stillness on him that was broken only as his hands lifted and hooked themselves on either side of the door; his forearms shook with the pressure of his grip, and then he struck a smashing flat-handed blow on the door jamb, made a strangling, cursing sound, and he wheeled and drew and fired all in one lunging motion.

Lanahan threw himself aside, the piercing thought within him: *God, Eileen's right behind him!* Then Flagg's bullet struck a terrible blow on his leg and dumped him in a graceless sprawl, with his arm twisted under him, the .44 like a gouging rock under his belly. Like a crippled animal he lashed and clawed and the .44 came out, dragging a track in the dirt with its muzzle; he lifted himself and brought the barrel into line and Homer's second bullet struck the hard-packed earth before him and the flattened slug struck his side, shocked him half blind and gagging for breath. The dismal thought was on him: *That does it...*

Hazily, almost dreamily, he saw Flagg's face, the raging, maddened pit-bull cast of his features. From behind Lanahan a keening tenor cry came.

'Flagg!' the voice cried, and Flagg's head lifted, and he fired again, not at Lanahan; above and beyond him; Lanahan heard the heavy thud of the bullet's impact. In that same instant Flagg was hit. His thick body jarred to the blow; there came another and another and another, in a steady, rhythmic *wham! wham! wham!* Shock came to Flagg's wide face at the second; he turned to the blow of the third; the fourth caught him turning, and he fell, pitching forward from the waist stiffly; the fifth shot jolted him as he fell. Through the thick cottony feeling in his ears from that close shocking sound, Lanahan heard the *snack-click-thack* of a hammer cocked and falling on an empty chamber.

'By God,' said Tennessee in a quiet wondering voice, 'I done shot up all my shells again.' He came into Lanahan's range of vision. He held the pistol as if it were very heavy, muzzle slanted down. He looked down at Lanahan with his tight glinting smile and narrowed yellowish eyes.

'That's six,' he said softly. 'You satisfied now, Clay?' Then his eyes widened and he made a soft sobbing sound of pain, dropped the pistol and fell against the side of the shack, hiding his face as he turned into that support. His legs gave under him, and he slid his shoulder down the rough logs unheedingly, twisting as he went, one leg doubled under, so that he sat in a cramped posture braced against the wall. 'God,' he said in a whispering voice. 'God, it hurts.'

Over by the lean-to Jed was crying like a hunting wolf, pleading with a terrible earnestness for somebody to just start something, begging them to make a move; a snarling gray wolf of a man with the Winchester lean and eager in his hands, spewing his rage at the mounted men who sat stiffly and watched him in naked fright.

''Tain't our fight,' one of them said. 'We just rode for him and done what he said.'

The whole violent thing had been done within seconds; Lanahan had a lulled dreamy sense of time stopped and waiting; but it had not been that way. From the time Homer Flagg wheeled and fired from the doorway until Tennessee's fifth bullet smashed his dying body perhaps ten seconds had ticked by; only now did Lanahan take his first full dragging breath, to feel it catch at him somewhere inside with a sensation of nerves being torn into ragged threads.

That pain cut through the shock like an icy douche; he still held his pistol clenched in his fist; he had fired one shot, he thought, but could not even guess where it had hit. He felt the .44 spill out of his fingers, with his left arm attempted to lever himself up; he made it part way, and Eileen came running, fell heedlessly to her knees on the packed earth beside him.

'Oh, Clay,' she cried, 'Clay!'

'I told you,' said Tennessee. 'You betteh marry that woman, Clay; good stuff in her.'

He hugged himself across the belly, with both arms; there wasn't any blood, where Flagg's bullet had hit; just an innocuous little hole in his shirt above the belt such as a man might burn by dropping a cigarette, or catching a coal popped from a fire.

'Ah,' said Tennessee, 'ah ...' He bent forward a moment, his eyes closed, then lifted his head, rested it against the wall behind him in utter tiredness. 'You hit bad, Clay?'

'Don't—know. Leg—up here some place.' The pressure was on him, the knowledge that the other riders were still there and therefore still a threat; he snarled harshly, 'Eileen, get out of this!'

'It's all right, Clay,' she said. 'It's all right.'

From somewhere, far away it seemed, he heard Jed's cry, 'Leave the buzzards have the big bastard ...' A little later, 'Load it up then, an' move damn easy ... I'm achin' ... now move on, and don't never come this way again ...'

Jed came and looked down at Lanahan, his face a block of carved gray stone. 'Oh, that big sonofabitch,' he said softly. He knelt, and turned Clay gently onto his back; Clay could look up into Eileen's face, and she was blinking rapidly; there was an oddly puckered smile on her face. Lanahan said, breathing shallowly because of the hurt in his side, 'Help Tennessee. He's ... hurt ... bad.'

'Never min',' said Tennessee, 'never min'.' His yellowish eyes went past them and lifted to look out through the draw and the open land beyond. 'Big country,' he murmured. Lanahan felt and heard the rip as Jed slashed the leg of his trousers with a sharp blade. 'Don't look like it busted nothin',' grunted Jed. 'Ma'am, you'll find a couple middlin' clean flour sacks in the shack.'

'Jed, he ought to have a doctor.'

'I'm goin',' said Jed, half irritably, 'soon's I stop this hole up.'

He bandaged the leg, and cursed himself when Lanahan grunted through locked teeth. That bleeding checked, he grunted,

'Better get him inside.'

Eileen helped him, and together they raised Lanahan, got him almost balanced, and then he sighed and collapsed and nearly pulled them down with him. Eileen cried out, and Jed said swiftly, 'He's just passed out. Better, anyway. He ain't hurtin'. Lemme have him.' He carried Lanahan, staggering under the load, into the cabin.

He came back out, and paused, looking down at Tennessee. 'Ol' hoss,' he said, 'can I do anythin'?'

'Go get that doctor,' said Tennessee. Jed wheeled, as if relieved, ran at a clumsy bowlegged gait to the corrals.

Eileen came and stood before Tennessee. She looked with concern at his deathly livid face and crouched before him. 'Oh, Tennessee,' she whispered.

From some inner strength he summoned a smile. 'Miss Eileen,' he said in a whispering voice, 'I wanta have somebody know. Don't want to be marked down for no thief. I was mad, when I rode out. 'Twasn't Clay's fault; he was right—but it was a while 'fore I thought—an' got oveh bein' mad. I knowed when Flagg seen you he'd go crazy—he'd kill Clay any way he could. So I come back.

'But I ain't no thief. I was maverickin'; the trader was payin' five dollars a head for slick-ears. Had me a pen, an' they was honest-to-god mavericks—not a brand on the bunch an' all past yearlin's. I come down this mornin', an' the pen was full of Flagg brands. Next thing somebody shot at me, an' I run; run my horse nigh to death an' shot up all my shells to slow 'em up when they winged me. But I neveh done it. I neveh stole them Flagg cows. You b'lieve that?' His yellow eyes were close and pleading on hers, and somehow she knew that this thing was more important to him than his mortal hurts.

'I believe you, Tennessee,' she said.

He breathed, in little gasping inspirations. 'That's good,' he said. 'You tell Clay, now.'

'I will,' she promised.

'He's a good man,' he said. 'Good a man as I ever knew.'

'I know that,' she said.

His yellow eyes fell searchingly on hers, and then a ghost of his old wicked grin showed. 'Miss Eileen,' he said, 'I purely wish I'd had somethin' betteh to offeh when I made my bid...'

'Oh, Tennessee,' she said softly, and reached out a hand and touched his face.

'Ah,' he said, 'thass ...' A blankness came on him, an incredulous bewildered look, and he fell against her. She knew as she touched him that he was dead.

* * *

The doctor had a big harsh voice, and he

looked a little like the pictures of General Grant; he said with a grim cheerfulness, 'I've sawed off a lot of legs that looked like that.'

'You're not sawin' this one off,' said Lanahan through his teeth.

'I hope not; I sincerely hope not. Now this other thing; superficial—superficial; some subcostal laceration, hemorrhage, simple costal fracture; nothing to it. The leg now, ...' He wore half-moon glasses, pulled well down on his nose. He looked over them at Eileen. 'Madam, is this man your husband?'

'No.' She was pale, but she was composed, and she had aided the doctor thus far without apparent qualm. 'No, he is not my husband.'

'Pity. A man shouldn't yell the way I'm going to make him yell except in the company of close friends or his immediate family. Ah, well.' He rooted through his capacious and evil-odored medical satchel, brought up a brown glass bottle, measured out liberal amounts into a basin of steaming water. 'Carbolic acid. Don't know what the medical profession would do without it. Whisky and phenol—the two standbys. Probably have to take up some honest trade like butchering hogs if we didn't have them.'

He found an instrument which looked much like an enormously long blunt-pointed needle. Through its big eye he threaded a strip of cloth, soused the whole thing in the carbolic acid solution.

'As an army surgeon, I found that a gangrenous wound almost invariably had some bit of dirty cloth or bullet patching or some such, within the wound itself. Seems a shame that a man has to wear a pair of dirty breeches when he does his gunfighting, but there it is.

'Ah, then. I'd say the material has had sufficient time to absorb the beneficial qualities of the solution. Now, madam—young lady—if he were a horse, I would suggest you sit on his head. Probably the next best thing in this case would be to hold his shoulders down. You,' to Jed, 'I shall want to hold his leg, thus, extended, and *hold* it. I don't want him kicking or jumping under this. You,' to Lanahan, 'hang on to the sides of the bed. If you wish to yell, do so. I have heard a good deal of yelling in my time.'

As he talked, he was busy. He tied a loose overhand knot in the threaded cloth strip; he knelt, with his angled thigh under Lanahan's thigh; at his last words he thrust the needle into the wound, probing slowly but firmly, thrusting all through the length of it from entrance to exit; with agonizing deliberation he hauled through the strip of cloth, one strong hand clamped above the wound, bearing down to hold it against his own bracing leg. Lanahan gritted his teeth, finally could not escape emitting one wolfish cry of pain that left him shamed and shaken; the doctor paid no heed, but dragged his torturing instrument through with cruel deliberation. Once through, he clapped a ready pad under the steadily bleeding, outraged orifice, signaled Jed with a jerk of his head, and placed the leg with a curious gentleness back on the rubber sheet which covered the lower end of the bed. 'Good man,' said the doctor cheerfully. 'I've known 'em to start yelling from the time I started the probe. Now then, another pad and a tight bandage, and barring gangrene, tetanus, and excessive hemorrhage, it probably won't bother you much more than if someone had struck you with an ax.' He fished a watch at the end of its chain from his vest pocket, picked up Lanahan's wrist, waited a contemplative half minute, snapped the watch closed. He said, 'Good boy. Strong as a horse. Young lady, I think both the patient and I could use some coffee. Young lady, you look a trifle peaked. Perhaps you had better step outside for some fresh air.'

'I'm all right,' said Eileen. Lanahan closed his eyes. He felt completely without strength, and his body was one great long screaming ache. He thought of Tennessee.

Tennessee was dead. Homer Flagg was dead. But why had Tennessee come back?

He hadn't really known Tennessee, he realized. He had never fully trusted him. Tennessee had been the lone wolf, with the mark of roving shadowy trails on him. He wished now he had known him better, had trusted and been trusted, for in his last few minutes of life, the man had been closer to him than a brother, and now he felt a terrible sense of loss.

Humility had a bitter taste. There had been something of Homer Flagg in himself; he had been stolid, brutal, unforgiving. There was something of Tennessee in him too; he had been wary, self-seeking, tough. But in the end, not as brutal or unforgiving as Flagg, for Flagg would have killed him without warning or mercy; nor as truly tough as Tennessee, who had come back. He knew he would always wonder if he'd have had the guts to stick his neck again into the noose as Tennessee had done. *Why had he come back?*

Lanahan came to with a start and saw the gentle worried look on Eileen's face as she bent over him. 'Can you drink this if I hold you up?' she asked.

'I can try,' he said. The coffee was black and strong and liberally sweetened, but a very little was all he wanted.

He lay back, looked at the ceiling, calling on all his stubborn patience to withstand his pain. Without looking at her, he said, 'Are you—sorry, about—Homer?'

'No,' she said low-voiced. 'No, I'm not sorry about him at all.'

'Ah,' he said. And then, 'Why'd he come back?'

'Who?'

'Tennessee. Why'd he come back?'

'He had to. He was your friend.'

'Better friend than I was to him. I shot off my big pious mouth and sent him off like a beggar.'

'He understood. He told me so.'

He rolled his head quickly, unmindful of his hurt. 'When? What did he say to you?'

She smiled at him. 'Before he—died. I'll tell you someday.'

The thought struck him then, and he demanded, 'Were you in love with him?'

She looked at him, with that look he knew so well, that cool and self-sufficient look, with somehow a hint of promise beyond it. 'Oh, Clay,' she said, barely murmuring it, 'sometimes you're such a fool.'

Her kiss rested on his lips as lightly as a feather. It too was cool, and waiting, and with a promise behind it.

'Eileen,' he said almost desperately, 'Eileen.'

'Hush now,' she said, and her lips were curved and red and close to him. 'Rest. The good times are still ahead.'

He slept, then, with her hand in his; and when he awoke, it was not to an end, but to a beginning.

Verne Athanas was born in Cleft, Idaho. His father was a construction foreman and so his growing years were spent constantly on the move, wherever his father's job happened to be. Schooling was sporadic although he did attend classes long enough in such places as an Oregon logging location designated simply as Camp 2 to learn how to read and write. In 1936 he married Alice Spencer and they came to reside in Ashland, Oregon. Writing was a career that came to him from necessity rather than design. At eleven Athanas was stricken by rheumatic fever that led later to the chronic heart disease which plagued his adult life. He began writing Western fiction for the magazine markets in the late 1940s. If there is a predominant theme in this fiction, it is the spectre of relentless determination required of a person in winning through in a life-struggle with the land and the hostile human environment in the American West. In his brief writing career, which spanned only fourteen years, he wrote only three novels but in them he sought to expand the conventions of the traditional Western and in *Rogue Valley* produced his masterpiece. In *The Proud Ones*, about a lawman and his handicapped assistant, he created a story which not only inspired a motion picture but also the long-running 'Gunsmoke' series on radio and then television. *Maverick* was his final novel, a cattle drive story which appeared originally in *The Country Gentleman*. Athanas died of a heart attack at the age of forty-four at a Western Writers of America convention in 1962. In addition to his legacy of three novels, many of his finest short stories are being collected into a single volume. In his concern for psychological themes in his Western novels and stories he was clearly in the tradition of Les Savage, Jr., Clifton Adams and T. T. Flynn and in his care for accuracy in historical detail he emulated the work of Oregon author, Ernest Haycox.